"I am not marrying some woman you've ordered from over the Internet!"

Gabe shouted the words at his twin brother.

Mike nodded in dejection and handed his brother a picture of a woman. A flight number was scribbled on the back. "Tatiana. Her name's Tatiana," he said. "Give her a chance, Gabe. You'll like her, I know you will. She's just your type."

Gabe took the picture but didn't look at it. He just wanted to get out of the office before he said or did something he would have to ask forgiveness for later. He didn't know when he'd ever been so angry. He wanted to get this woman and her daughter back on the plane and forget this had ever happened. It was too bad she'd have to be disappointed, but what kind of woman would agree to marry a man she didn't know, anyway? She'd pulled the wool over his brother's eyes, but she wouldn't fool him.

COLLEEN COBLE and her husband, David, raised two great kids, David Jr., and Kara, and they are now knee-deep in paint and wallpaper chips as they restore a Victorian home. Colleen became a Christian after a bad car accident in 1980 when all her grandmother's prayers finally took root. She is very active at her church where she sings and helps her husband with a Sunday school class. She writes inspirational romance because she believes that the only happily ever after is with God at the center. She now works as a church secretary but would like to eventually pursue her writing full-time.

Books by Coleen Coble

Don't miss out on any of our super romances. Write to us at the following address for information on our newest releases and club information.

Heartsong Presents Readers' Service
PO Box 719
Uhrichsville, OH 44683

From Russia with Love

Colleen Coble

Heartsong Presents

For Mary Rhoads, true sister of my heart.

A note from the author:
I love to hear from my readers! You may correspond with me by writing: **Colleen Coble**
Author Relations
PO Box 719
Uhrichsville, OH 44683

ISBN 1-58660-164-4

FROM RUSSIA WITH LOVE

Cover illustration by Ron Hall.

one

Tatiana Lazarenk buried her hands deep in the pockets of her ragged coat, but the threadbare wool was little comfort. She set her trembling chin. Swallowing hard, she blinked against the sting of tears. She wouldn't cry. Weariness slowed her movements, but she squared her shoulders and slogged through the snowdrifts. Her thin shoes gave no protection from the Russian cold.

Stopping outside the small house at the end of the street, she stomped the snow from her feet and pulled her hands out of her pockets to open the door. The piercing cold of the wind numbed her fingers almost instantly. Pushing open the door, she stepped out of the wind. A shiver trembled through her, and she shut the door.

The small house smelled of urine and garbage. Her shoulders drooped with fatigue and hopelessness. If only there was someplace else for Irina to stay. Then she heard her daughter's voice, and her despair lifted. She followed the sound of the gentle voice she loved so much.

"Is it time for *Mat* yet?" Irina asked. "I want *Mat*."

"Quit asking for your mother." The woman's voice was so gruff, she nearly sounded like a man.

Tatiana winced at the impatience in Olga's voice. Stepping into the room, she held out her arms. "Where is my lamb?" The sight of her daughter's corkscrew curls lightened her heart. As long as Tatiana and Irina could stay together, things would be all right. But how long would that be? She pushed away the persistent question.

"Mat!" Irina's blue eyes lit up at the sight of her mother. She slid from the chair and ran to Tatiana.

Tatiana swept her up and hugged her. Tatiana's eyes stung again at feeling Irina's small bones through her skin. Although she would be four in four months, she looked more like two. She struggled to keep the despair from her voice. "Were you a good girl today?"

"Very good." Irina wrapped her arms around her mother's neck. "You're cold, *Mat.*" She buried her face in Tatiana's hair. "You smell like *borshch.* Can we have *borshch* for supper?"

"She's a handful, that one," Olga said. "I want my money, or don't bother bringing her tomorrow. If you want charity, take her to the orphanage down the street." Her beady eyes squinted. "I know you got paid today."

Tatiana's heart squeezed with fresh pain. Not the orphanage, never the orphanage. But the fear that the gray building at the corner might one day be her only answer loomed larger every day. She swallowed. "Klara was able to pay only half what she owed me." She hated the way her voice quavered. Where was her pride, her determination? The grinding poverty had worn it thin. If he were still alive, Sergio wouldn't believe his spitfire wife could have so little pluck.

By a supreme effort, she squared her shoulders and faced Olga's stare. "Can you wait for half until the first of the week? Irina must eat, Olga."

"That's not my problem," Olga sniffed. "I want my money, or you can find another one to take care of your brat."

Irina tugged on Tatiana's hair. "I'm not a brat, *Mat*. I was very good," she whispered.

"I know you were, my lamb." Weariness pierced more deeply than the cold wind. She was so tired of fighting to survive. She had to have a place to bring Irina tomorrow, or she couldn't work. There was no choice. She put her daughter down and dug into her pocket. Clutching the meager coins a moment, she sighed, then dropped nearly all her money into Olga's hand. As she slipped Irina into her small worn coat, Tatiana felt hopeless tears well up in her eyes. What could they do for food for the next few days? And what if Klara couldn't pay her the rest of her wages on Monday? There were no answers to the questions. She swallowed hard and carried Irina through the door and into the wind-driven snow.

The drifts had worsened in the short time she was inside Olga's house. With Irina in her arms, Tatiana struggled for nearly half an hour to reach their small flat. Opening the door, she put her daughter on a chair and lit a lamp. Their electricity was erratic at best and had been out for two days. The meager light illuminated the tiny room occupied by two cots, a washstand, and two chairs. She wrapped Irina with a blanket, then hurried to light a fire in the stove. Within minutes, the little room was warm enough for them to take off their coats. She warmed some milk for her daughter and smoothed a bit of butter over the last slice of bread. It would have to do for Irina's supper.

Irina was nodding sleepily by the time she finished the last of the milk and bread. "Bedtime for you, my angel." Tatiana slipped Irina into a flannel gown and tucked her in the small cot near the stove. "Sweet dreams."

"Sweet dreams to you too, *Mat*," Irina murmured.

Tatiana hid her sudden surge of tears. Her dreams were likely to be punctuated with nightmares of how to feed them both. Hunger gnawed at her belly, but she was just glad Irina wouldn't cry of hunger tonight. She washed the few dishes and went to check the mail. Someday their luck would change. She clung to that hope, but it grew dimmer every day.

Why had Sergio gone to that demonstration? Because of his fervor, she was alone. And poor Irina didn't remember her father at all. She'd been only a year old when he was killed.

Tatiana opened the door and retrieved the mail. A few bills and a thick envelope. Her hunger forgotten, Tatiana stared at the envelope. From America. Her heart pounded. Could this be someone who had seen her picture on the Internet? Was this a way out for her and Irina?

Her hands trembling, she tore the envelope and stared into the man's handsome face. His gray eyes seemed kind, but maybe that was wishful thinking. Opening the typed letter, she scanned it, glad her English was so good. Her heart soared. Someone *was* interested in her. She read the name again. Gabe Salinger. A strong name. Where was Indiana? She would have to look at the atlas in the library.

Terror and exhilaration fought for control of the tightness in her throat. To leave this familiar place was frightening. But allowing her daughter to grow up in this deprivation terrified her more. She was willing to do anything for Irina. Anything at all.

Wait until she told Oksana! Her friend would take full responsibility for the news, as well she should. Without her persuasion, Tatiana would never have done such a crazy thing. With this letter in her hand, it suddenly didn't seem so crazy. She had resisted the idea at first, but watching her child suffer had stifled any sense of pride she had. The threat of the orphanage made anything else seem a lifeline of hope.

⁂

A month later everything had changed. She was going to America! There would be food for Irina, nice clothes, and a home. Mr. Salinger had flown to Russia to meet her. Though he struck her as a bit too carefree, he was a blond, very handsome man of thirty-two. She had hoped to find someone more mature and stable, but no one else had answered her ad. It was this chance or none. She wondered why such a handsome man found it necessary to get a mail-order bride instead of finding someone in America. But she hadn't wasted much time on the thought. She was just thankful he was only five years older than she was and not lecherous. He'd been a perfect gentleman.

She filled out the biographical data for her fiancée visa and went to the doctor's examination. The tensest moment came when she realized the police would have to give her a letter saying she had no criminal record. Would they hold Sergio's demonstrations against her? But the police made no mention of that. Perhaps Mr. Salinger's influence had smoothed the way.

Tatiana had packed their few belongings, given notice at work, and informed her landlord she would be vacating the flat. Tomorrow she and Irina would leave this dreary flat for the last time. She pushed away the knowledge that she would be back in ninety days if Mr. Salinger decided not to marry her. She had just put Irina to bed when someone knocked on the door. Who would visit so late? She peeked through the peephole. Her mouth went dry when she saw her sister-in-law.

Arranging her face in a welcoming smile, she opened the door. "Polina! How lovely to see you!" She hadn't seen Polina in over two years. Not since Tatiana's brother Anton, sweet, generous Anton, had been killed. Her eyes still filled with tears every time she thought of her older brother.

Polina's eyes were fearful, but she settled herself on the threadbare sofa and took Tatiana's hand. "I got your letter last week. I couldn't let you leave with harsh words between us." Tears spilled down her cheeks. "Please forgive me, Tatiana."

The apology broke her heart. "I'm sorry, too. When Anton was killed, I had to blame someone. I know it is not your fault the police killed him. It was his fault for going to that worship service when he'd been forbidden to go."

"Are you still angry with God?" Polina asked gently.

Tatiana bit her lip but couldn't hold back the bitter words. "What kind of a God would take everyone I love from me? What kind of a God would allow my brother, such a kind and gentle man, to die because he wanted to worship Him? What kind of a God would allow my daughter to cry in the night because she was hungry? Tell me, Polina. Is that the kind of God anyone should worship?"

Tears slipped down Polina's cheeks, and she shook her head. "My sister, you must let go of this anger. This bitterness will ruin your life. God loves you and wants you to come to Him. You mustn't marry this man in America just to escape. You don't know anything about him. There is so much violence in America. What if he is some sort of murderer who preys on women? You had love with Sergio once. Don't settle for second best."

Tatiana shook her head. "Don't talk to me of God. He hasn't cared that we are cold and hungry. I must find my own way to take care of Irina. I will learn to love this man. And violence is even more widespread here. We will be fine."

Polina gripped her hand. "I am so afraid for you."

"Be afraid for yourself. You are in for much pain and disillusionment from your God."

Polina touched Tatiana's cheek. "My dear Tatiana, I fear you are the one who will find disillusionment. But I will be praying that God will send someone into your life who will show you His love."

Irina awoke at the voices, and the women changed the subject. Tatiana knew Polina would never see how futile her faith was. Just as Anton and Sergio had never seen.

The next morning the alarm went off at four, but Tatiana was already awake. She had barely slept. After pulling on a moth-eaten sweater and worn slacks, she dressed Irina. Mr. Salinger had left them some money, and she had considered buying some new clothes, but prudence had prevailed. What if they were sent back to Russia? She must hold onto any money she had.

One large, battered suitcase held all their possessions. The flight would be long and tiring, but America beckoned at the end. Tatiana couldn't help the thrill of hope. They had a chance at a better life—only a chance—but it was better than none at all. It was better than the orphanage.

Through the window of the bus, she gazed upon the dirty streets of St. Petersburg for the last time. A lump grew in her throat, but she forced it away. All she was leaving behind was hunger and deprivation. All those she loved were gone except for Irina. What awaited her in this faraway place called Indiana? She would soon find out.

ು

"Will you quit pacing! What is wrong with you? You haven't been able to sit still for three days. Sit down and tell me so I can get some work done." Gabe pushed back his chair and propped his feet on his desk. It was likely woman trouble again. Women were all his twin brother Mike seemed to think about.

Mike stopped his pacing and turned to stare at Gabe. His face was pale, and he dropped his gaze. "You're probably going to kill me when you hear." He fiddled with some papers on Gabe's desk. "I've regretted doing it, but it seemed the only way to introduce you to life. I thought I had to do something. When was the last time you asked someone out? Bet you can't even remember."

Gabe frowned. "What have you done now? I suppose it's that woman you're seeing. What's her name, Letitia? The one with black hair and clothes. Even her nail polish was black. She could pass for a younger Elvira." He was used to getting Mike out of scrapes, but he had hoped his brother was beginning to settle down. He'd even asked out a really nice young lady last week. Margaret Baxter was an accountant, very stable and levelheaded, who attended Gabe's church. She'd talked Mike into attending with her last week.

Mike groaned and leaned his head into his hands. "I haven't seen Letitia for a month. I like Margaret. A lot. She's the one who said I had to tell you and give you a bit of warning. She said I deserve anything you do to me."

Gabe thumped his chair forward and put his feet on the floor. A flicker of alarm disturbed him. He'd never seen his twin so agitated over a scrape of any kind. It must be worse than usual. He sighed. "Let's hear it."

"I was surfing the web a few weeks ago after you'd been on me to find a nice girl and settle down. It was just before we went to St. Petersburg, remember?"

Gabe nodded. "You weren't much help in Russia. Every time I turned around you were off somewhere."

Mike dropped his eyes. "That's part of it," he said. "Anyway, I found this site offering mail-order brides from Russia. The conditions are so bad there, many women are desperate to escape. It was rather pitiful, actually."

"You didn't order yourself a bride!" This was the absolute limit. Gabe wanted to throttle his brother. Well, he would just have to live with the consequences this time.

"Worse," Mike said, "I ordered you one."

For a moment, Gabe only stared at his brother. Mike's hair stood up on end where he'd raked his fingers through it, and he was pale. He was also serious. Gabe opened his mouth but no words came, so he closed it again. He gulped and tried again. "You ordered me a bride. From Russia."

He stood and walked to the window and looked down onto Canal Street. Their business, Salinger Architects, was in a prime building in the downtown area. A snowstorm had covered Wabash with eight inches of snow, and there was very little movement below. Bewilderment slowed his thoughts. His mind wouldn't quite grasp what Mike had just said. Surely, he'd heard his twin wrong. As through a fog, he heard Mike continue the eager recitation of his latest debacle.

"She's really nice. Her name is Tatiana, and she's a widow with a three-year-old daughter. They were destitute and barely had enough food to survive." Mike's voice was eager as he tried to further explain the situation.

A woman was coming here with a child and expected *him* to marry her! Gabe wheeled back around. "How? Just tell me how you could order me a bride? That certainly sounds illegal to me!" His voice rose nearly to a shout. He raised his hands as he stepped toward his brother, then forced himself to drop them back to his sides. If he wasn't careful, he could easily choke Mike. *Control,* he told himself. *Don't lose control.*

Mike licked his lips. "I—uh, I gave her your name. We *are* twins, you know. I filled out all the paperwork in your name. I had a picture taken with her; but since you and I look alike, no one questioned that it was a picture of you and her together. I had to show them your Russian visa to prove you'd been in Russia. My friend Jeff works for Immigration, and he ran the visa through for me quickly as a favor."

"So she has no idea that she's not marrying the man she met?" Gabe's voice rose again as the full impact of what his brother had done hit him. "We have to stop her from coming!"

"It's too late. Her plane arrives at Indy in four hours."

Gabe lost his voice. He wanted to grab Mike by the shoulders and shake him. How could he do something so irresponsible? His eyes squeezed to slits.

"Go ahead," Mike said, "call me all the names you want. You can even swear at me, and I won't tell your pastor. I deserve anything you say or do. Let go of that ironclad control of yours for once. It would make me feel better."

Gabe dropped into his chair. His knees felt shaky from the effort to maintain the control on his composure. "I don't want to make you feel better. And if I lost that control you like to make fun of, I would pound you to a pulp." He didn't know how he was going to straighten this mess out. "I'm not telling Mother. You have to tell her yourself."

Mike's eyes widened. "Not that, Gabe. Anything but that. She'll just look at me with those sad blue eyes, and I'll feel like an absolute heel."

"You are a heel. Did you for one minute stop to think about this woman and her child?" He stood to his feet and put his hands on his hips. "How they would feel when they found out they had to go back to Russia?" He forced himself to drop his hands, but he had never wanted to hit something so badly in his life.

"I think you'll like her," Mike said eagerly. "The other women on the website listed their measurements and were dressed in sexy clothes with lots of makeup. She was dressed in a conservative dress that went nearly to her ankles and very little makeup. Her ad said she was interested in a stable man who loved kids and wanted a family. She's really beautiful but in a classy way. Her hair is so blond it's almost white, and she has the deepest blue eyes I've ever seen. You can see she's suffered a lot, though. She has to be married in ninety days, or she'll have to go back to Russia."

"I am not marrying some woman you've ordered from over the Internet! I don't care how nice or how beautiful she is." Gabe rose and picked up his coat. "You tell Mother what's happened and why I have to miss dinner. I'll go pick up this Tatterina or whatever her name is and put her back on the plane to Russia."

"Tatiana," Mike corrected.

"Whatever." He shook his finger in Mike's face. "But this is the last scrape I'm getting you out of!"

Mike nodded in dejection and handed his brother a picture of a woman. A flight number was scribbled on the back. "Tatiana. Her name's Tatiana," he said again. "Give her a chance, Gabe. You'll like her, I know you will. She's just your type."

Gabe took the picture but didn't look at it. He just wanted to get out of the office before he said or did something he would have to ask forgiveness for later. He didn't know when he'd ever been so angry. He wanted to get this woman and her daughter back on the plane and forget this had ever happened. It was too bad she'd have to be disappointed, but what kind of woman would agree to marry a man she didn't know, anyway? She'd pulled the wool over his brother's eyes, but she wouldn't fool him.

two

The plane engine whined as the pilot throttled back in preparation for the landing. Tatiana craned her head to peer through the small window for her first look at Indiana. Snow blanketed the ground, and she could see the lights of a large city spread out below. Indianapolis, she assumed.

Her seatmate Mildred, a white-haired lady with a sweet smile, leaned toward Tatiana and patted her hand as the plane taxied to a stop at the terminal. "I wish you well, my dear," she told Tatiana. She stood and dragged her bag from the overhead compartment. "If you're not met, have me paged. Wabash is on my way home to Warsaw."

Tatiana smiled her thanks at the older woman, then stood and stretched. After plane changes in London and again in New York, she felt stiff and sore. Irina was a deadweight against her shoulder, her mouth open as she slept soundly. Kind Mr. Salinger had not seemed to mind the added expense of a little girl. Her heart warmed with hope at the thought.

She stood and waited as the people filed past. She wasn't in a hurry herself. She dreaded seeing Mr. Salinger again. He'd been a gentleman in Russia, but now she was on his soil. She'd heard horror stories from other families who had sent a daughter to America. The idea of meeting Gabe Salinger again sent a wave of fresh dread through her. No one here cared about her. He could do whatever he wanted, and no one would know.

The plane was nearly empty, so she squared her shoulders, then lifted Irina into her arms and went down the aisle to the ramp. The terminal teemed with people, and Tatiana didn't see her future husband at first. She shifted Irina to the other arm and looked around. What if he had changed his mind and didn't come? What would she do? She had his address but not his phone number. The small amount of money she had wouldn't get her and Irina very far.

Then she spied his blond head towering over a rotund man. Her mouth dry, she started toward him. He still hadn't seen her as he scanned the crowd. She stopped a few feet from him and waited for him to see her. His shoulders were broader than she remembered, but he was just as handsome. His square jaw seemed more trustworthy and dependable than she'd remembered. There was a strength and purpose about him that surprised her. In Russia, she'd thought him a bit flighty and irresponsible. Her gaze paused on his cleft chin, and she wondered again why such a handsome man found it necessary to find a wife on the Internet.

He shifted from one foot to the next as he scanned the crowd. His gaze met hers, and his gray eyes widened. He cleared his throat. "Tat—uh?" he asked uncertainly.

Had he forgotten her name already? She stared at him for a long moment. "Of course. You did not recognize me?"

Tatiana stared up into the stormy gray eyes of the man she'd agreed to marry. Still puzzled at the differences she saw in him, she took a step closer. It was in the way he held his shoulders and the firm line of his lips. Maybe things would be all right, after all. Maybe he would be someone she could lean on and depend on. She smiled tentatively.

"Glad I am to see you." Should she kiss him? She studied his eyes and took a step back.

He frowned and took her arm abruptly. "We need to talk." He steered her to a secluded corner and sat her in an empty seat. As he stood towering above her, she settled Irina against her shoulder and rubbed her aching arm muscles. She longed for a warm shower and a place to rest. The long trip and the time difference had taken their toll.

"Please. Can you sit? My neck aches to look up at you so high."

He stared at her a moment, then nodded and sat in the seat beside her. Why did he stare at her so? It was as if he'd never seen her before.

"What's your daughter's name? I've forgotten."

He'd forgotten? Tatiana didn't like the sound of that. She wanted a husband who would love Irina, too. So far, this meeting hadn't turned out at all like she'd hoped. "Irina. Her name is Irina Natalia Lazarenk."

He nodded. "I, uh, I need to talk to you."

She nodded. "Yes. Already you say this." A growing feeling of unease constricted her throat.

He cleared his throat. "I know you think you came here to marry me, but I've never seen you before in my life."

Tatiana frowned. What did he mean? Of course, he'd seen her. They'd had a lovely lunch in St. Petersburg. "I–I do not understand," she stammered. She was too tired to think. The hustle of the airport terminal distracted her, and she couldn't get her thoughts corralled enough to understand what he was getting at.

He sighed and pressed his lips together firmly. "My crazy brother wants to see me get married. He was the one you met in Russia. He gave you my name and filled out all the paperwork with my name on it. I didn't know you were coming until four hours ago."

Tatiana gulped. A shaky foreboding started deep within her. This wasn't the man she met in Russia? How could that be?

"Mike and I are twins. Not many people can tell us apart." He answered the unspoken question before she could ask it.

Tatiana's stomach churned, and she felt suddenly faint. He was about to send her back to Russia. She knew it was so by the look on his face. There was a touch of contempt in his eyes mixed with an unwilling pity. She opened her mouth to speak, but no words came out.

"Have you had anything to eat? The least I can do is feed you before you go back."

Go back. He intended to send her back. Back to deprivation and hunger for Irina. Back to the cold one-room apartment. She laid a hand on his arm. "This is—this some kind of joke?" she asked. "I cannot go back, Mr. Salinger. I came here to be married. My job and my home, both are gone. There is nothing to go back to." She wrapped her anger around her like a blanket. She must fight, for Irina she must be strong. Gathering her strength, she straightened her shoulders. She must not let him intimidate her. Their entire future hung in the balance.

Gabe frowned, and she saw a touch of uncertainty race over his features. The sight gave her hope, but then he stared at her and shook his head.

His glance softened when he looked at the sleeping child, then hardened again when he met Tatiana's gaze. "I don't know what to say. I have no intention of marrying a woman I don't know, despite my brother's whims. Of course, I'll help you get back and pay to get you started again. But I don't even know you. How could we marry?"

Tatiana felt the blow to her soul, felt his utter contempt for her. How could someone marry a stranger? He had only to live in her shoes for one day. How would he feel if his child went to bed without dinner? If she cried out in the night for food? Would he be so quick to judge then? She would not accept this answer, though she longed to creep away from the disdain she saw in his eyes. For Irina's sake, she *could* not slink off like a naughty child. She had done nothing wrong.

She dug in her purse and pulled out the letter. "I was promised! I am not, how do you say, a coin scooper!" Tatiana stiffened her spine. She saw his lips twitch, and anger flooded her.

"Gold digger," he corrected softly. "You're not a gold digger."

"That is what I say! I am glad you can finally see this." She wanted to slap his smiling face. "I do not deceive your brother. He is one who deceived me!" How could he and his brother do this to her and her daughter?

Gabe's grin faded, and he stared at her then nodded. "True, he did. And I guess I owe you something for that." He flipped open his checkbook and began writing. "How about if I give you a thousand dollars and pay for your way back to Russia?"

Tatiana jumped to her feet with Irina in her arms. "No! I do not wish for your money. I want what I am promised!

A home for Irina and me. Look at my daughter! She is only three and cries in hunger many nights. You cannot send me back without giving me the chance."

"She's right."

They both turned at the voice. A tiny woman of about sixty with white hair and startling green eyes stood facing them. She wore green slacks with a green paisley blazer that deepened the color of her eyes. The look in those eyes told Tatiana the lady was used to having her own way.

Gabe stood. "Mother! What are you doing here? Don't tell me you're in on this, too."

Mrs. Salinger turned her direct gaze on Tatiana. "Introduce me, please, Gabe."

Gabe's shoulders sagged, and he shrugged. "Mother, this is Tatiana. Tat–Tatiana Lazarenk and her daughter, Irina. Tatiana, this is my mother, Grace Salinger."

Mrs. Salinger took Tatiana's cold hand in her own. "I'm delighted to meet you, my dear. You must call me Grace. Mike told me about the situation, so I came as quickly as I could to see if I could help straighten it out. I can see I arrived just in time."

Tatiana searched the woman's eyes and thought perhaps she had found an ally. Could this woman keep her son from sending her back to Russia? "Please," she said with an outstretched hand, "can I not stay for at least the ninety days I was promised? Maybe I find a job and earn money to keep us if we must go back."

"Of course you can, my dear girl." Mrs. Salinger turned to her son. "She will stay with us in the guest house, Gabe."

"But, Mother—" Gabe began.

With an imperious wave of her hand, Mrs. Salinger

silenced him. "You are not to bully her, Son. It is unthinkable that we would allow Mike to deceive her so and not make some effort to make amends. We can surely find someone in need of such a lovely wife."

Gabe stared at his mother, then back at Tatiana. When his gaze touched Irina, his face softened, and he shrugged. "I suppose you're right."

He raked a hand through his hair and glanced at Tatiana again, confusion clouding his gray eyes. He obviously blamed her for the situation. But why did he blame her and not his brother? This Mike was the one who should be ashamed, not she. Could he not see she was not this gold-digger type of person?

"*Mat.*"

Tatiana looked down as Irina called for her mother in Russian. Irina's round face was flushed from sleep, but her bright eyes looked around with interest. Tatiana smoothed the hair back from her daughter's face tenderly. "Did you have a nice sleep?" she asked in Russian.

Irina nodded. "Is that my new *otets?*" She still spoke in Russian. Staring up at Gabe, she reached out a tiny hand to grasp the brass buttons on his navy blazer.

Gabe's granite expression softened as he looked at the child. "Hello."

Tatiana was glad for the many nights this past year she'd spoken English to her daughter. Irina could speak English almost as well as she did Russian. She was quite precocious for almost four.

Irina stared at him. " 'ello, Daddy," she said in English.

The tenderness on his face vanished, but Tatiana thought there might have actually been a quick flash of longing before he whitened and stepped back. She was heartened at the thought.

"We need to go," he growled.

Irina's blue eyes widened at his gruff tone, and she burst into tears. Tatiana hugged her close and soothed her. "It's okay, my lamb," she whispered in Russian. "He wasn't talking to you."

"Gabe!" Mrs. Salinger grasped his arm and shook it. "Mind your manners. You've frightened that beautiful child."

Gabe sighed, then turned and strode away. Tatiana watched him go with tears in her eyes. She should have known things would not work out for Irina and her. They never did. Not for her.

ða

Gabe fumed as he strode toward the concession stand. He needed coffee. He couldn't think clearly. The events of the past four hours had totally perplexed him. How was this all his fault? He was an innocent victim, yet even his own mother looked at him like he was a villain. That woman was the one who'd agreed to sell herself to some man she didn't even know. He could have been a murderer or a thief or some other kind of scoundrel. She had no business bringing a child halfway across the world into a situation she knew nothing about.

A more uncomfortable thought surfaced. She was the most beautiful woman he'd ever seen. Her long hair curled around her shoulders in a loving embrace. She was about five four and slim. Really too slim. He'd have to fatten her up a bit with good, nourishing food. He caught where his thoughts were drifting. He must be mad. She was just a beautiful gold digger, as were all gold diggers, most likely. But her daughter was darling. Thick blond tresses that hung in corkscrew curls down her back. Big blue eyes like her mother's and a dimpled smile. Just the little girl any man would want for a daughter. He felt a shaft of regret and focused on his anger at her mother.

Several minutes later, he'd calmed down. He would be polite but nothing more. Mike and his mother wanted this Tatitia or Tatiana, or whatever her name was, here, so *they* could dance attendance on her. He would tend to his business and keep to himself. The ninety days would be over soon. And maybe he could soothe his conscience by helping find her a husband.

Since his mother's diabetes had worsened, and she'd come to live with him and Mike in the family home, she had been bored. This would give her a project. Somebody he knew must be desperate enough to take the woman. As he walked back to find his mother and the Russian woman, he tried to compile a list in his head of his unmarried friends who might be interested in her. Her beauty would attract some poor sap. But it wouldn't be him. And she didn't really seem money hungry. After all, she'd turned down the thousand dollars he'd offered her. Maybe things were bad enough in Russia to warrant such desperation.

His mother sat beside her and her child in the corner where he'd left them. Why couldn't he remember her ridiculous name? What was it again? Tat something. He glanced at the back of the picture Mike had given him. Tatiana. Tat and Anna. Tatiana. He rehearsed it in his mind a few times until he was sure he had it right, then strolled up to the women. "Are you ready to go?" He lowered his voice and smiled. He didn't want to frighten the child again.

Little Irina cowered against her mother's shoulder when she heard his voice. His conscience smote him at the little girl's fear. Kids usually loved him. He knelt and spoke softly to her. "I'm sorry I sounded so mean. I have something for you." He dug in his pocket and pulled out a miniature candy bar. "Here." He offered the brightly wrapped candy to her, but she hid her face.

Tatiana searched his face, then took the candy from him. "*Spasibo*. Thank you." She spoke to the child softly in their own language. She opened the wrapper, broke off a piece of chocolate, and popped it into Irina's mouth. Tatiana smiled when her daughter's face lit up.

"You're welcome," he said. Irina reached out and touched his face with her small fingers, then hid her face against her mother's shoulder again. Gabe grinned and stood.

"Why don't I bring the car around while you and Tatiana find her luggage?" Grace Salinger stood and pulled on her coat.

Gabe nodded. "We'd better get going. I'd like to get home before it gets to late. Do you have your luggage tags?"

Tatiana dug in her pocket and found her ticket stub with her luggage tag attached. "Here. There is only one." She handed it to Gabe, then rose with Irina in her arms.

Gabe felt an unwilling admiration for her poise and dignity. She'd rolled with the punches pretty well today. He'd have been happier if she'd agreed to go back to Russia immediately, but at least she didn't seem the type to cause a lot of trouble for his mother.

"Do you think Irina would like to come with me?" Grace asked.

Tatiana's arms tightened around her daughter, but when she saw the gentleness in Grace's eyes, her tense shoulders relaxed. She spoke gently in Russian to Irina, then handed her to Grace. The little girl went willingly enough and stared up at the older lady with round blue eyes. She reached up and patted Grace's white hair.

Gabe suppressed a grin. Mother hated to have her hair messed up.

But, surprisingly, she didn't seem to mind as she cuddled Irina and headed toward the escalator. "I'll meet you at the baggage terminal," she called over her shoulder as she went.

Gabe couldn't help but watch Tatiana's face as he led her through the terminal. The Indianapolis International Airport was clean and well lit with many beautiful shops and lovely tiled floors. He remembered the ancient Moscow airport he'd been in just two weeks ago and knew she had to be contrasting this airport with the ones in her country. Expressions of wonder and awe flashed across her face as they passed the fast-food places and shops. No wonder the shops were so full of overpriced trinkets. It didn't take much to impress people who weren't used to such abundance.

She saw him looking at her and shrugged. "Never have I seen so many things to buy," she said. "In my country, it is hard just to find food to buy. It is much to understand."

"You ain't seen nothing yet," he said. He flushed at her look of incomprehension. "I mean, you haven't seen anything yet. There are many stores and shops in every town. My mother will enjoy showing you around."

"But not you." The words were not a question, but a statement.

Gabe shrugged. "I didn't have any choice in the matter. If it were up to me, you'd be on the next plane back to Russia. But I love my mother, and her health has not been good. Maybe you'll be good for her."

"You will not give me a chance to show I can be a good wife?"

"I don't want a wife. I'm perfectly happy with my life the way it is." Okay, well, maybe he was a bit dissatisfied, but he wasn't about to admit it to her. He saw his friends with cozy homes, wives, and children—and sometimes wished he could find the right woman for himself. But it certainly wouldn't be a mail-order bride his brother had ordered for him. What would people think? Did Mike think he was such a poor catch he had to get a wife who'd never met him? And he didn't know how she felt about God. He wanted a wife who loved the Lord like he did. Mike just had not been thinking when he concocted this harebrained scheme.

Tatiana didn't answer his pronouncement that he didn't want a wife, and he was glad she dropped the subject. It made him feel like a worm squirming on a hook to know he could do something about her plight.

He stepped onto the escalator, then realized she wasn't with him. He turned and looked behind him.

She stood clutching the handrail, her eyes wide with terror. "I cannot."

He bounded back up the slow-moving escalator to where she stood. "Hey, it's okay. It's just an escalator." He saw her shoulders shaking with fear.

"I know what it is. Russia is not primitive. These conveyances we have, too. But even in Russia I cannot ride on one. The terror, it rises up and I freeze."

He laid his hand on her trembling shoulder. For just a moment he wanted to sweep her into his arms and comfort her. What was wrong with him? It was as though Mike's revelation that morning had addled his brain. He wasn't reacting properly to anything. "It's okay. We can take the stairs." He pointed to the set of stairs a few feet away.

By the time they found her baggage, nearly half an hour had passed. He wondered if Mother was getting impatient. He grabbed the suitcase and strode toward the door with Tatiana trailing him. He heard the purr of the engine of his mother's gray Chrysler LSD as the terminal's doors slid open. She popped the trunk as soon as she saw him, and he tossed the suitcase in the trunk and slammed the lid.

The window on his mother's side slid down noiselessly. "Mike brought me down, and I had him take your car home so we could travel home together. Do you want to drive?"

"Sure." Just so he didn't have to chitchat with the Russian woman. She made him feel like a heel, which was probably exactly what she wanted. Once this trip was over, he could bury himself in the office and leave her in his mother's hands.

His mother opened the car door and clambered out. He slid behind the wheel while she settled in the backseat. Tatiana slipped into the seat right behind him, and he could feel her staring at the back of his head. Gabe just wanted this trip over and the woman safely ensconced in the guest cottage where he didn't have to see her or think about her. And when he got his hands on his brother, he was going to throttle him.

three

Tatiana's eyes burned with unshed tears. It was hard to talk past the lump in her throat. Mrs. Salinger—Grace—as she insisted Tatiana call her, pointed out things along the way as they drove back to Wabash. Tatiana tried to pay attention, but her thoughts were in such a whirl, it was hard to concentrate. What difference did it make that America was beautiful, even covered in snow, or that there were wonderful shops and huge supermarkets and malls everywhere she looked? She wouldn't get to stay and enjoy it. Irina wouldn't be allowed to enjoy it. She cast a glare at the back of Gabe's head. Why wouldn't he give her a chance? Perhaps he would find he liked her if he let himself get to know her. After all, she had been a good wife once.

He was so smug and safe here in his homeland; she didn't know if she even wanted to marry someone so hard and uncaring. He would have put her and Irina back on the plane without another thought if it hadn't been for his mother.

Irina, buckled into the seat belt beside her, leaned against Tatiana's side. Grace asked her about her life in Russia, and she told her about her job as a cook, about Sergio's death, and the way they'd lived. Grace had fallen silent, finally, and the hum of the big engine was seductive. Tatiana's body ached with weariness. Maybe she'd just close her eyes for a bit herself. Her eyelids drooped as she settled back into the leather seat.

Tatiana woke with a start. The car was no longer moving, and she realized the press of her daughter's warm body was gone. She jerked upright. "Irina!"

"It's okay," Grace said soothingly. "I've got her. We're home." She opened her door and handed Irina up to Gabe. "Take her up to the old nursery, Gabe," she said.

He frowned. "I thought they were going to stay in the guest house."

Grace sent him a look of reproof. "Not on their first night here."

Gabe's lips tightened, but he didn't say anything. He took the sleeping child and carried her toward the house.

Tatiana swung her stiff legs out of the car and stood on weak knees, which wanted to buckle under her. She stared in awe at the front facade of the house. A wide porch, flanked on each side with massive white pillars, swept the front of the three-story brick mansion.

"One house this is?" she whispered. Trees lined the long driveway they'd just come down, and the home seemed to be nestled in a small woods. Tatiana couldn't hear any other cars. The only sounds were birds twittering on the nearby trees. Surely they weren't in a city?

Grace tugged on her arm. "Come along, dear. You'll be frozen in no time with this wind."

Tatiana allowed herself to be pulled along the brick sidewalk and up the steps to the massive double doors. A huge brass lantern porch light swung above her head in the wind. She snapped her mouth shut when she realized it was dangling open.

Grace pushed open the door, and Tatiana followed her inside. Her mouth gaped again as she stepped inside the entry. Brilliantly colored mosaic tile formed a Victorian urn pattern on the floor. A cream wallpaper embossed with the same urn pattern covered the walls. The ceiling, oh, the ceiling! Tatiana had never seen a ceiling like it. It was like looking up into the sky. Clouds drifted across the blue expanse, and cherubs adorned the corners. She stood and gawked.

Beyond the entry, she spied what was obviously a library with massive walnut shelves that lined gleaming wood floors. On the other side of the entry, she could see into the enormous living room. It was elegantly furnished with antiques and overstuffed furniture that cried out to be sat in. What must it be like to live in a home like this? Tatiana swallowed hard as Gabe came down the sweeping open stairway. She must find a way to keep Irina here.

"Irina didn't even wake up when I put her in the bed," he said. "I could use a Pepsi. Anyone else want one?"

"Would you ask Martha to fix us some tea?" Grace shrugged out of her coat and hung it in the coat closet. She held out her hand for Tatiana's coat.

Tatiana took it off. "Please, I can hang it myself. You must not wait on me."

Grace took it from her with a smile. "It's been too long since I've had a young girl to fuss over. The last time was when my niece lived with us for a year while my sister was overseas." She frowned as she looked at the coat.

Tatiana felt a wave of heat creep up her neck and onto her cheeks. What must Grace think of her? She knew how it looked. Two waifs with threadbare coats, few possessions, and worn shoes turning up on the doorstep of such a wonderful mansion, almost a castle. Did Grace think she was a gold digger, like Gabe said? Tears of humiliation stung her eyes. These people were much too wealthy. She could never fit in here. She might as well get on the plane and go back to Russia.

Grace touched her hand. "Don't fret about things now, dear girl. Come into the parlor and we'll have some tea. I know you must be exhausted."

Tatiana followed her into the large room and sat in the chair by the fireplace. She looked down at the beautiful Persian rug on the floor. Her shoes, laced with numerous holes in the soles, looked out of place on the obviously expensive rug. Grace sat in the chair beside her and kicked off her leather pumps.

A thin, bird-like woman with frizzy red hair came through the door at the back of the room. She carried a delicate blue and white teapot with matching cups on a tray.

"Missus, you shouldna been out on these roads," the woman scolded. She placed the tray on the carved coffee table in front of the chairs. "Now you drink some hot tea and warm up. I brought you some cookies, too. They're still warm."

Grace smiled. "Thank you, Martha. I'd like you to meet Tatiana Lazarenk. Tatiana, this is Martha Wells. She's been my friend and housekeeper for going on thirty years. Tatiana is going to be staying with us for a few months, Martha. Her three-year-old daughter, Irina, is asleep in the nursery."

Martha sniffed. "Just so long as she doesn't dig up my flowers. Little ones can be terrible destructive. My rose-bushes still suffer from what those two hoodlums of your brother's did to them last year."

"Irina will not bother anything," Tatiana said hastily. "She is a good child. And we will be in the small house for guests."

Martha's stiff shoulders relaxed a trifle. She turned to Grace. "Would you like me to pour?"

"No, no, you go along and finish dinner. I'll pour. Where's that son of mine?"

"Which one? Mike dropped Gabe's car off and lit out of here like he had a fire on his tail. Gabe is raiding my refrigerator and whining about being hungry. I told him dinner wouldn't be more than a half an hour, but he thought he had to have something now. I took pity on him and gave him a couple of cookies, too." Martha walked back toward the far door. "I'll tell him you're looking for him."

Grace nodded, then poured the tea into the two cups. "Sugar?"

Tatiana hesitated, then nodded. She hadn't had sugar in so long she could hardly remember what it tasted like. Even tea was a distant memory. She eyed the cookies and found she was suddenly ravenous. She took the cup Grace handed her. The cup looked fragile, so she handled it gently. She closed her eyes and breathed the aroma as she sipped the tea. It was heavenly to roll the sweet liquid around on her tongue.

The door opened again, and Gabe strolled into the room. Tatiana's breath caught in her throat at his sudden appearance. His broad shoulders seemed to fill the room.

He dropped onto the couch and stretched his long legs in front of him. "Mike seems to have turned tail and run. I don't think he wants to face Tatiana."

Grace shook her head. "I've scolded him, too. And he deserves anything Tatiana says to him."

The thought of what Mike had done broke the contentment that had cocooned Tatiana. She hadn't yet thought about what she would say to Mike. She dreaded the inevitable meeting. Did he have any idea of what a terrible thing he'd done to her?

"Have a cookie." Gabe's deep voice interrupted her thoughts.

She looked at the plate of cookies he was holding out. They looked delicious. All she and Irina had had to eat for so long had been bread with some occasional soup or potatoes. She picked one up. It was still warm.

"It's chocolate chip," Gabe said. "My favorite."

She bit into the cookie, and the rich, chocolaty sweetness flooded her mouth. Her eyes widened. She'd never tasted anything so wonderful. Her stomach growled, and she hurriedly swallowed. She took another bite of the cookie, then put it down on her saucer.

He cocked his head. "Don't you like it?" There was a faint frown between his eyes.

She hurried to reassure him. "It is wonderful," she said. "But Irina will like it, too. I will save some for her."

His frown deepened. "There's lots more where those came from. Martha made a huge batch of them. The cookie jar in the kitchen is full, and Irina can have all she wants. And so can you. Go ahead. Eat it."

Hesitantly, she picked up the cookie and stared at him. "Truly, there is more for Irina? I would not want her to miss this good food."

"Lots more. I promise."

She stared up into his gray eyes. He seemed sincere. Hesitantly, she ate the other half of the cookie. She tried not to wonder how long it would be before she and Irina were back to eating only milk and bread.

Martha thrust her frizzy red head through the door. "Dinner's ready. You want me to wake up the little one?"

"I'll get her." Tatiana stood quickly, and a few crumbs fell from her skirt to the floor. "*Nyet!* Oh, no." She'd spoiled the carpet. She frantically began to pick up the crumbs with her fingers.

Grace tugged on her arm. "My dear girl, don't worry about it. Martha will get it when she vacuums."

Tatiana reluctantly got to her feet. She felt terrible about messing up the carpet. She was so clumsy. "Where am I to find Irina?" she asked. Grace looked at Gabe.

"I'll show you," he said. He stood and led the way up the wide, sweeping staircase.

Tatiana ran her hand along the gleaming wood as she followed him. The surface felt smooth and luxurious under her fingertips. Her feet sank into the plush Oriental runner in the wide hall upstairs. She lost count of the doorways they passed until Gabe stopped at one and opened the door for her.

A Winnie-the-Pooh theme decorated the large room. Irina lay snuggled under a Pooh comforter, and the brightly colored Pooh wallpaper lifted Tatiana's spirits immediately. Irina would love this room. A tiny rocker sat in one corner, and a Pooh toy chest overflowing with toys sat against one wall. Even in Russia, the fat yellow bear was popular with the children. She'd never been able to buy Irina one, though.

"How wonderful," Tatiana breathed. It was like a storybook room. What must it be like for a child to grow up in a room like this where every item, every stick of furniture, oozed careful thought and love? Irina deserved to find out.

Gabe grinned. "Mother has kept this same theme since we

were small. I was always the Pooh bear, and Mike was Tigger. Our personalities still kind of reflect that. Mike rushes in where angels fear to tread, and I'm always hungry."

Tatiana couldn't repress the smile that came to her face. She remembered what Martha had said about Gabe raiding the refrigerator.

"You grew up here?"

He nodded. "When Dad died, Mother decided she wanted a condo in town. Mike and I kept the big house. But since her health has not been good, she's come back for a while. Once she gets her diabetes under control, she'll probably go back to town. She's very independent."

He was kind to his mother. That was a good sign. Walking to the bed, Tatiana pulled back the covers. "Irina," she whispered, "wake up, my lamb."

The little girl's eyelashes fluttered, and she peered sleepily up at her mother.

"Are you hungry?"

Irina seemed to consider this question. "*Da*," she said with a nod. She sat up and put her arms around her mother's neck.

Grace was seated at the table when they entered the elegant dining room. Tatiana glanced around quickly at the large walnut table, the lovely trinkets, and the dishes in the two china cabinets. Another Oriental carpet was on the floor here, too. How much money did these people have? Tatiana couldn't begin to imagine.

"Please sit beside me," Grace patted the seat to her left. "Martha has brought in Gabe's old high chair for Irina."

Tatiana cast a surreptitious look at Gabe. She couldn't imagine this self-possessed man ever being a child. She sat

Irina in the walnut chair and pushed it up to the table. She didn't need the tray, so Tatiana left it on the floor beside the chair and slid into the seat beside Grace.

The aroma of the food made her mouth water. Steaming plates of food covered the white tablecloth. Tatiana's wondering eyes saw chicken, potatoes, several types of vegetables, hot rolls and butter, gravy, and salad. She couldn't believe the magnificence of the feast. Did they eat like this all the time? She waited hesitantly to know when to begin.

Gabe cleared his throat, and Tatiana's gaze flew to his face. He and Grace bowed their heads, so Tatiana did, too. Were they praying? Yes, they were. They didn't see her shocked expression. Hesitantly, she bowed her head and closed her eyes.

Gabe's deep voice filled the room. "Lord, we thank You for this bounty before us and for Martha's dear hands that prepared it. Bless it to the nourishment of our bodies. In Jesus' name, amen."

Unconsciously, Tatiana clenched her hands in her lap. Not Christians! Were they everywhere she turned? Anger welled up in her. Gabe Salinger was too pious to marry an immigrant but not too pious to bring her from Russia as a practical joke. She ignored her conscience that whispered it had not been his doing.

She opened her eyes as Gabe picked up the platter of chicken. "Would Irina like a drumstick?" he asked.

Tatiana stared at him. There were no drums here. What did he mean?

A teasing smile lit his face. "You don't know what a drumstick is?"

Tatiana shook her head and felt the hot tide creep up her

cheeks. She had been so proud of her English. It seemed very inadequate to her now. Gabe picked up a chicken leg with the tongs and leaned across the table to put it on Irina's plate.

"A drumstick," he said. "All kids love them."

Why did they call a leg a drumstick? It made no sense to her. She avoided his eyes, took the platter of chicken from him, and selected a piece.

Tatiana tried to be dainty and ladylike as she ate. She didn't want Gabe or Grace to know that this was more food than she'd ever seen in her life. She was a bit embarrassed by Irina's obvious enjoyment of the meal. She kept smacking her lips as she shoveled the food into her little mouth. Gabe's lips quirked up several times at the loud noises emanating from his old high chair.

"Let's take our dessert in the family room," Grace suggested.

Tatiana followed Grace and Gabe into another room near the back of the house and off the kitchen. It was smaller than the front room and not so elegant. Comfortable dark green leather chairs and sofa circled the room, and a huge television sat in one corner. Fat candles that gave off a delightful aroma of cinnamon and apples burned on the coffee table.

Tatiana perched on the edge of the sofa and put Irina down beside her. Gabe and Grace each took an overstuffed chair as Martha wheeled in a dessert cart.

Grace insisted she try several different kinds of dessert. Tatiana wanted to pinch herself to see if this evening could really be true. How wonderful it had been to see Irina eat until she was full. She didn't even eat any dessert except for half of a cookie. Tatiana herself felt as though she wouldn't be hungry again for days. It would have been a perfect evening if she had thought it would last. And if Gabe hadn't stared at her so much through the entire evening. Tatiana couldn't read his expression. Did he still think she was a gold digger?

The back door clicked shut, and Tatiana heard muffled footsteps go across the kitchen.

"Sounds like Mike is back," Gabe said.

Tatiana sucked in her breath and looked at the floor.

Gabe stared at her for a moment. "I've got an idea," he said. "How would you like to give Mike a dose of his own medicine?"

Tatiana looked up and frowned. "He is sick?" Maybe that was why he had done such a terrible thing to her and his brother. She tried to find a particle of pity for him but couldn't.

Gabe grinned. "I mean, how would you like to get a bit of revenge? I need your help to do it, though. Come with me, and follow my lead."

By the time they caught up with Mike, he had one foot on the staircase.

"There you are, Mike." Gabe's voice stopped Mike, and he turned slowly and came back down into the foyer.

He looked quickly at Tatiana, then flushed and looked away. "Sorry I missed supper."

"I was just telling Tatiana how glad we will be to have her in the family. She'll make you a wonderful wife."

Mike paled. "W–wife?"

Tatiana glanced quickly up at Gabe. *He'd said no such thing,* she thought indignantly. He wanted to send her back to Russia. When she saw the twinkle in his eye, she realized it was a joke. This was much too serious a situation for joking; couldn't he see that?

"She's going to stay in the guest cottage until the wedding, but you need to start looking for a place for the three of you to live," Gabe said casually. "Sharing the house was fine for you and me, but I know you'll want to start your new life in your own place."

Mike was already looking shaken. And he deserved to be disturbed. She would shake him up more. "Oh, my darling, so glad I am to see you again. Your brother has told me you asked him to pick me up because you were so frightened. I am sorry I got your name wrong." She gave a little laugh and stepped closer. Mike, his eyes wide, backed up against the railing. "So silly I was to think your name was Gabe, but your brother has corrected me. The good wife I will be to you. You will not be sorry you brought me over to marry you." Her accent was pronounced as she cornered him against the banister.

The look on Mike's face said volumes. His eyes were wide with panic, and he paled even more. Tatiana told herself he deserved to feel the panic she had felt at the airport. She wouldn't feel sorry for him. Maybe it would teach him responsibility in the end.

Mike cast a desperate look at Gabe. "Uh, ma–marry you?"

"When?" Tatiana gave him her most bewitching smile. "I am ready now."

Mike reached behind him and gripped the railing. Tatiana stepped closer. He tried to sidle away, but she threw her arms around his neck.

"Gabe," Mike gasped, "do something."

four

Tatiana couldn't still the stab of triumph as she got into bed. Mike had smiled a sickly grin when he realized they weren't serious. Her smile faded. It would have been nice if Mike had realized the responsibility he had to her and Irina. His relief had been a bit humbling. Of course, she knew she was no great catch. With Irina, her husband would have two mouths to feed; but she would work, too. She didn't expect anyone to give her a free ride.

Tomorrow she must try to make some kind of plan. She never wanted to see Irina want for a meal again. The bounty of America only reminded Tatiana that there was enough to go around. Going back to Russia would mean failure, and she couldn't fail. Someone out there would want her. Perhaps she might be a housekeeper in trade of marriage. She had to think of something.

At the thought of her daughter, she slid out of bed and padded down the hall to Irina's bedroom. The little girl was asleep in the middle of the bed. Tatiana sighed. She doubted her own sleep would be so peaceful. Odd how Irina had shown no fear of her new surroundings. She'd even warmed up to Gabe once she realized he wasn't going to eat her. Their nightly English practice had been well worth the effort. Irina had slipped into speaking English in a most amazing way.

Tatiana backed out of the room and turned to go back to

her own bed. A shadow loomed over her. Her heart racing, she stepped back.

"It's only me." Gabe's deep voice rumbled in a near whisper.

If that was supposed to make her feel better, it didn't. She swallowed the lump in her throat. What did he want now? For a few lighthearted moments when they'd teased his brother, she'd thought him almost human. Until she remembered he wanted to send her home. She eyed him warily.

"Is she okay?" He peered around her at the sleeping child.

Was that really concern in his voice? She licked her dry lips. "She sleeps."

"Good." Gabe hesitated a minute, then cleared his throat. "I'll let you get some rest." He stared at her a moment, then turned and walked to the other end of the hall where he disappeared inside his own room.

Tatiana shook her head and hurried back to her room. She shut the door firmly behind her. The fewer dealings she had with Gabe Salinger, the happier she would be. What had made him stop to check on her and Irina? Could he have a softer heart than she'd seen so far?

Pulling back the covers, she put on her nightgown and crawled into the bed. The comfort of the bed was unlike anything she'd ever known. Smooth sheets caressed her skin, and it actually had a blanket that heated the bed. She'd heard of such things but never seen one before. Only the very wealthy could afford such luxuries in Russia.

Burrowing under the covers, she breathed the fresh aroma and sighed happily. No wonder Irina had fallen asleep so quickly. In spite of Tatiana's resolve to consider her options, her eyelids dropped, and she slept.

જ

Sunlight streamed through the window and touched Tatiana's face. She awoke disoriented. Where was she? Irina's small body was not snuggled next to her for warmth. Panic gripped her throat until she remembered. Smiling, she stretched, then slipped out of bed. Her bare feet sank into the plush carpet, and she wiggled her toes with delight. She would check on Irina, then shower.

She pulled on her ragged robe and opened her door. Her nose twitched at the aroma of bacon from downstairs. If that didn't awaken Irina, nothing would. Slipping down the hall, she peeked into the nursery. Her daughter still slept, her cheeks rosy in sleep. Tatiana smiled and hurried back to her room to shower.

She had just pulled on her jeans when she heard a shriek. Throwing open the door, she rushed out into the hall with her hair hanging in wet strands around her face. She collided with Gabe. He reached out a hand to steady her, and they both rushed to the top of the steps. A crumpled form lay at the bottom of the stairs.

"Martha!" Gabe took the steps two at a time with Tatiana close on his heels.

"Oh, no!" Grace came from the living room doorway and ran toward the housekeeper.

Gabe reached her first. "Mother, call for an ambulance," he said. "Don't touch her. The fall may have damaged her back."

Grace drew back her hand hesitantly and looked up into Gabe's face.

"Hurry!" His firm tone did not invite discussion.

Mike came running down the steps with his face still lathered with shaving cream. "What happened?" Pushing by Tatiana, he knelt beside the housekeeper's still form. He brushed the frizzy red hair back from Martha's face.

"Don't move her," Gabe ordered again. "Mother has called an ambulance. They should be here in a few minutes."

Martha moaned and rolled her head.

"Lie still," Gabe said urgently. He laid a hand on her head to quiet her.

Tatiana eyed him uncertainly. His gentleness surprised her. In the few hours she'd known him, he'd seemed so stern and unbending. She pointed to Martha's leg. "Her limb. It is broken."

Gabe looked where she pointed and bit his lip. "It certainly is," he said. "A compound fracture." The leg stuck out in an awkward way, and the bone had broken through the skin.

The wail of the siren echoed in the distance, then grew louder as they all crouched over Martha. Her eyelids fluttered once, but she moaned and lapsed back into unconsciousness. Within minutes the ambulance arrived, and Grace ushered the paramedics inside.

They loaded Martha onto the stretcher, and she opened her eyes. "I'm sorry, Missus," she whispered. "I don't think I'll be cooking for your dinner party."

"Don't fret about it," Grace soothed. "It's not important."

"It's your birthday party," Martha murmured.

"And I'll survive without a party." Grace patted the housekeeper's shoulder. "I'll follow the ambulance."

Martha nodded and closed her eyes. The paramedics

carried her out, and Grace sighed. Hurrying to the closet, she opened it and took out her coat. "I don't know when I'll be back. You boys don't even have your breakfast."

"I will cook the breakfast," Tatiana said timidly. Her face grew warm at the stare Gabe turned on her. Did the man think she didn't know how to cook? Then she saw the knowing look in his eyes, and her face became hotter. He thought she had an another motive. Did he think she was so determined to trap him, she would use poor Martha's circumstances?

Grace's face brightened. "Thank you, dear. Ask Gabe to show you where everything is." She took her purse and hurried out the door. "It smells like the bacon is done, at least."

Gabe frowned at Tatiana. "I can fix my own breakfast," he said.

"So can I," Mike echoed.

Tatiana shivered at the cold air that blew in the door and crossed her arms as though girding for battle. "Your mother said I was to do it."

Mike shrugged. "So she did. Are you sure you won't poison me?"

She narrowed her eyes. "You deserve it, Mr. Salinger. But the poison I left in Russia."

He grinned. "I guess I can live with Mom's lack of faith in my ability to fend for myself."

"I must check on Irina first."

"I'll fetch her," Gabe said.

Tatiana stared at him doubtfully. "She will be frightened."

"No, she won't. Let me show you the kitchen first." Whistling, he strode toward the kitchen without giving her a chance to reject his offer.

Tatiana bit her lip, then followed him. She paused at the door, and her mouth dropped open. The room was a gleaming display of high-tech equipment from the professional stainless steel range to the double refrigerators. The granite counters invited her to run her fingers over them, and she obliged. The slick, smooth surface made her itch to roll out dough for Russian black bread.

Gabe went to the closest refrigerator inside. "Here are the eggs. An omelette is good enough." He swung open a bottom cupboard and whirled the lazy Susan. "I'll fix the toast. You shouldn't be waiting on us like this." He paused and stared at her.

She sensed the doubt in his gaze and tilted her chin up defiantly. "I am capable of preparing breakfast."

His gray eyes softened, and he smiled. "I'm sorry if I made you think I doubted that. We got off to a rocky start, Tatiana. My only excuse is that I was blindsided by Mike just before we met. I know that's not a good excuse for my bad manners, but I hope you'll forgive me."

"Blindsided?" she asked uncertainly. "You cannot see on one side?" She had taken English classes, but these people came up with words she'd never heard.

He chuckled. "That means he came out of left field and surprised me."

"Left field?" She still didn't understand.

His grin broadened. "Forget it. But I am sorry. Can we start fresh?" He thrust out his hand. "Friends?"

She took his hand gingerly. His large hand enveloped hers, and a shock of awareness ripped through her. His gaze snagged and held hers, and she caught her breath.

"Fri–friends," she stammered.

His eyes darkened, and he released her hand abruptly. "But that doesn't mean I've changed my mind. Mike had no right to put us both in this situation. But I'll do what I can to help you find a husband, if that's what you want."

"It is not so much what I want, as much as it is necessary." Tatiana turned away so he couldn't see the hurt in her eyes. For just a moment she had hoped he *had* changed his mind.

"I'll get Irina," he said after a long pause. "The toast will be done in a minute. Can you butter it?"

She nodded and turned to the refrigerator. She heard his steps go to the door and down the hall. Breathing a sigh of relief, she took out the tray of eggs and rummaged in the refrigerator for omelette ingredients. The food supplies nearly took her breath away. It would be a joy to cook in a kitchen like this. She found cheese, fresh mushrooms, and sausage. She would make the men an omelette they would talk about for weeks.

By the time she heard Irina's voice in the hall, the omelettes had cooked up fluffy and moist, the toast was done, and she'd set the kitchen table with bright yellow plates she found in the cupboard.

"Mat, Mat!" Irina ran into the kitchen, calling out to her in Russian.

"Good morning, my lamb." Tatiana spoke in English. Irina needed to adjust as soon as possible, and the best way was speak to her only in English.

Irina's forehead wrinkled in concentration. "Good morning," she said carefully. She lapsed quickly into Russian. "Daddy brought me a cookie. But I am still hungry."

Gabe's head turned when he heard the little girl say daddy. His gaze met Tatiana's, and she saw the alarm in it. She wanted to tell him that Irina didn't really know what the word daddy meant—to her it was just a name—but she held her tongue. Irina didn't need to be more confused by explanations.

"Breakfast is ready," she said. She lifted her daughter to the high chair and put some omelette and half a slice of toast on a plate for her.

Gabe slid into the chair beside Irina and gave a sigh of appreciation. "Smells good. Looks good, too." He bowed his head and prayed silently.

"Where is Mike?"

"He'll be along. I suspect he's waiting until he's sure I'm in here so he doesn't have to face you alone."

Tatiana gave a slight smile. "He does well to fear me. But I will not harm him now. I am no longer angry. At least Irina is warm and has food."

Gabe's smile faded, and his gray eyes looked down.

Regret curdled her stomach. She shouldn't have said that. He would think she was trying to make him feel guilty. But it was the truth. For ninety days Irina would be warm and well fed. That was worth something. Perhaps she would have more strength to face the life that waited them in Russia if they had to go back.

Mike entered, and she turned a smile on him. At least she wouldn't have to be alone with Gabe. Mike's gaze dropped, and he bit his lip.

"I'm starved," he said. He dropped into the chair at the end of the table.

Tatiana poured both men a glass of juice and a cup of

coffee, then started to wash the dishes she'd dirtied in cooking.

"Aren't you eating?" Gabe asked.

"I will eat when you are through," she said.

He stood and came toward her. Taking the dishcloth from her hands, he took her arm and led her to the table. "You're much too thin," he said. "Join us while it's still hot."

His gaze was intent and kind. Tatiana's shoulders relaxed, and she nodded. "Very well." His concern brought a warm glow to her stomach. She sat on the other side of Irina. With jam smeared around her mouth, the little girl had nearly demolished her breakfast. She smacked her lips in satisfaction and ran sticky fingers through her hair. Tufts of blond hair mixed with purple jam stuck up from her head. She looked like a tiny punk rocker. With meals like this every day, maybe she would soon look her age. Right now, she looked like she was less than two years old.

Gabe grinned. "I think she got more jam on her than in her."

Tatiana relaxed at his smile. She had been afraid he would think she had not taught her daughter manners, but he must have been around enough children to not be put off by their messiness. "This is the first time she has eaten jam. I think she likes it."

"If she liked it any better, we would have to invest in a vineyard just to keep her happy," Gabe said.

Tatiana's heart warmed at the fondness in the glance he gave Irina. "What shall I do today while everyone is gone?"

"Hmm, I guess it will seem odd to be here alone. Mother should be back in a few hours. You could just explore the house, maybe take a nap." Gabe stood and went to the sink to wash his hands.

They were trusting her with their beautiful things. "Might I go to see the city?"

He frowned. "I rather you wait until one of us can take you. I wouldn't want you getting lost."

"The bus I could take."

He grinned. "I can tell you've never been to the States. There are no buses except in large cities. Here in Wabash, it's a car or hoofing it."

"Hoofing it?" Where did he get these phrases? Did all Americans talk in riddles?

"Walking. Hoof, like a cow's feet. Get it?" Mike explained.

"Ah, I see." But why could he not merely say what he meant? The slang confused her. "I will not get lost. I shall walk to town. Just direct me."

Gabe sighed. "It's too cold to walk. You'll get a chance to see the town soon."

His resigned tone stung. Did he consider her so much a burden? She turned her head so he wouldn't see the tears that smarted her eyes. The tears angered her; she wasn't usually so weak. "Very well," she said.

He stared at her, but she refused to look at him. Shrugging, he walked to the doorway. "I'll be back around twelve-thirty. Mother will likely have returned by then. Have her call me and let me know how Martha is doing if she returns before I do. When I come back, I'll take you for a sight-seeing trip."

Mike followed his brother. "Uh, see you at supper." He still refused to meet her gaze.

Moments later, the front door slammed, and Tatiana sniffed. Left alone on her first full day in her new country. It seemed unfair. Her daughter's condition caught her eye. The first thing on the agenda was a good scrubbing for Irina. She scooped her up out of the chair and carried her upstairs.

There was a bathroom attached to the nursery. Tatiana gasped when she stepped inside. The tub was almost like a child's pool, inset with Winnie-the-Pooh figures. The washbasin and toilet were small and set low to the ground for a child's easy access. She'd never seen or heard of anything like it.

Irina clapped her hands. "Look, *Mat*. I take a bath." She began to pull her nightgown over her head.

"One moment, my lamb. Let me fill the tub with water." Tatiana turned on the spigots and found thick towels with Pooh trim in the cabinet.

Irina danced with anticipation. Once her mother gave her permission, she pulled off her clothes and hopped into the tiled tub. The sides were low enough for a child to get in and out easily.

Tatiana found shampoo and rinse on the side of the tub. She scrubbed the jam from Irina's thick curls. Once her daughter was clean, she let her splash and play a bit, then coaxed her out with the promise of a walk when her hair was dry.

She hated to dress Irina in the tattered overalls, but they were the best she had. Irina's hair was still soaked, and she went to find her blow dryer. Her own hair was still damp and could use the fluffing a dryer would give. But when she tried to plug her dryer in, she discovered the plug wouldn't work.

"Outside, *Mat*. I play in the snow." Irina danced around impatiently.

"Not with wet hair," she told her. Did she dare look in the other bathrooms and borrow a dryer? Grace had told her last night to make herself at home and to use whatever she needed. She glanced doubtfully at Irina. Her thick tresses would take all day to dry without help. In sudden decision, she started down the hall. The first bathroom was clean and spotless, but also empty of any personal effects. It was obviously for guests. The next room was Gabe's.

Tatiana hesitated with her hand on the doorknob. Would he feel violated if she entered his room? He would never have to know. She would replace the dryer when she was done. With resolve, she turned the knob and pushed inside the room. Standing on the threshold, she gazed around. Neat and tidy, the room was large with huge windows that looked down onto a basketball court. The massive bed was walnut and masculine even with the half canopy over it. Pictures of magnificent buildings decorated the walls, and she remembered he was an architect. He must love his work.

"*Mat*, see!" Irina ran to a marble-top dresser and reached up. Exquisitely detailed building figurines clustered atop the dresser. Irina couldn't quite reach them.

"No, Irina. Don't touch," she said sharply. They were obviously expensive. She picked her daughter up so she could see them. "They are Gabe's. We mustn't bother them." Her heart sank at the knowledge that Irina would be sure to talk about them. Gabe would know they had been in his room. She should never have come in.

It was too late for regret now. She set Irina on the floor and took her hand. Leading her into the bathroom, she found a black dryer on the wall. Even Gabe's bathroom was neat, his shaving gear lined up along the top of the counter, the used towel from this morning neatly folded and lying across the tub. She sniffed. The scent of his aftershave stirred something deep inside her. It had been so long since she'd been in a man's domain.

She shook herself out of her reverie. Briskly, she fluffed Irina's curls and dried her hair, then her own. Hanging the dryer back in its place, she took her daughter's hand and hurried from the room. She had best forget she was ever here. This glimpse into Gabe's personal life was too enticing.

five

Gabe found it hard to concentrate on his blueprints. His thoughts kept drifting to Tatiana's deep blue eyes and the dimples in her cheeks. It had been so long since he had been around a woman who appealed to him as she did. He shook his head. Mike had outdone himself this time. He would be hard-pressed to top this snafu. He glanced at his brother's shut door. At least he was ashamed of himself. He was often unrepentant when caught in a bind. Maybe it was Margaret's influence.

The clock chimed. Eleven o'clock. Mother should have called by now to let them know Martha's condition. Maybe that was why he was so antsy. He would surely feel better if he knew how Martha was. He had put his hand on the phone to call the hospital when the phone rang.

"Gabe." His mother's voice was strained, and his heart sank.

"How is she?"

"Bad. She's in surgery now. She'll be in the hospital several days, but luckily there was no spinal damage. She has two cracked ribs, too. I don't know when I'll be home. Not until sometime this afternoon, I'm sure. Could you call the guest list for Friday and cancel?"

"You sure you want to do that? You've been looking forward to seeing your friends for weeks. Major MacGregor will be in town only another week."

Grace sighed. "I don't want to do it, but I don't know what else to do. Martha will need me, and you know how impossible it is in Wabash to find catering."

"Do you suppose Tatiana can cook?" He bit his lip. What a stupid suggestion. He wanted to get her out of their lives, not more embroiled.

"Hmm, she did say she was working in a restaurant before she came. Would you ask her?" The hope in his mother's voice made him feel worse. He was thinking about his own comfort instead of his mother. Her seventieth birthday should be a joyous event.

"I'm taking her around town for lunch. I'll talk to her about it." It was too late to back out now. He just hoped she could deliver after he'd gotten his mother's hopes up.

"You are?" His mother's voice grew alert. "She's darling, isn't she?"

"Now, Mother, don't go matchmaking. She's not the right one for me."

"How do you know? She might be a Christian. You haven't given her a chance yet. I should dearly love to have Irina for a granddaughter." Her voice was wistful.

He gave a short bark of laughter. "You'd like to have *any* grandchildren."

"But you have to admit that child is special."

"Yes," he said grudgingly. "But I can't marry a woman just to get her daughter."

"I suppose not." His mother's voice trailed off. "Here comes the doctor. Pray for Martha." She hung up, and Gabe replaced the receiver on the hook.

He prayed for Martha and the doctors, then grabbed his coat. It was early, but he couldn't concentrate. He might as well go home and check on Tatiana and Irina. He told his secretary he'd be gone a few hours and hurried to his car.

The February wind bit through his coat, and he shivered. Snow drifted across the road and piled along the curbs, but he drove carefully and had no problems. He was glad he'd told Tatiana not to walk. It was much too cold for her to have the little girl out. The driveway was full of snow, but his Jeep bit through the drifts and climbed the drive with no problem. He set his brake and jumped out of the car.

The homey aroma of fresh-baked bread teased his nose when he opened the door. From the scent it seemed she could cook. He followed the fragrant smell to the kitchen and found two loaves of some kind of dark bread. He touched one. It was still warm. He wandered around the house calling her name. Silence was all that answered him. He frowned. Where could she be?

He walked back into the entry and found a note on the stand. He scowled. She'd gone for a walk. He'd told her to stay inside, and she had gone outside, after all. Crumpling the note, he tossed it into the wastebasket. He marched to the door and stepped out into the wind.

He found large and small sets of footprints and followed them. They led to the road and away from town. The fool woman was taking Irina in the wrong direction. A small voice reminded him that she didn't know which way was toward town. But that was all the more reason she should have listened to him and waited until he could take her.

He jumped into the Jeep and whipped around the circle driveway. Driving slowly, he followed the tracks down the road. Rounding a curve on Mill Creek Pike, he saw two figures in the distance. There they were. He eased the

Jeep up behind them.

Tatiana, her bare legs peeking from under her skirt, kept marching straight ahead, Irina's hand clasped in hers. When he slammed the door, she seized Irina in her arms and whirled to face him. Her terror eased when she saw him. Her lips trembled, but she tried to smile.

"I told you to wait. Town is back that way." He jerked his head to the north.

"I was about to turn around," she said. "We were just taking a walk."

"I told you it was too cold out."

She laughed, and he liked the musical sound of it. "This is not cold. It is much worse in Russia. We are used to the cold, Irina and I. Besides, you do not have any right to tell me what to do."

She was right; he didn't. The thought was galling. And indeed, the little girl's cheeks were pink, and she looked happy and content. She reached out her arms for Gabe, and he took her without thinking. Her little coat was worn and threadbare. The frayed ties on her hat barely managed to tie under her chin. This child needed some new clothes. He saw Tatiana's coat was in the same condition and made an instant decision.

"I'm taking you to lunch. Get in the Jeep." They would have lunch, and he would take them shopping, whether she liked it or not.

She tilted her chin. "You did not ask if I had plans."

She was a feisty little thing. He suppressed a grin. "Fine. Would you like to accompany me to Wabash for lunch?" He wouldn't tell her about the shopping yet. She would just get stiff-necked again.

She inclined her head graciously. "I should enjoy it."

He turned and started back toward the Jeep. Buckling Irina into the seat belt, he realized the first item needed was a car seat. Tatiana waited to see that he had taken care of her daughter, then went around to the passenger side and slid into the seat. Her gloved hands clutched her battered purse, and she stared resolutely out the window.

"Daddy, I am hungry," Irina announced.

"We're going to go eat now, sugar," he told her. He wished she would quit calling him daddy. It filled him with a strange mixture of longing and fear, as though some kind of mystery awaited him. One he wasn't sure he was ready for.

They were all silent for a few minutes as he drove the five miles to town. He glanced at Tatiana from the corner of his eye. She sat erect with her perfect carriage, her head high and a remote expression on her lovely face. "I'm sorry," he said gruffly. "I had no right to try to dictate to you."

She sniffed. "You did not. I am a woman, not a child to be ordered about."

"I said I was sorry, okay? You're supposed to say you forgive me." He was growing nettled by her stiff demeanor.

She shrugged. "Very well. I forgive you."

"You could say it like you mean it."

She twisted in the seat belt and turned to face him. "You treat me like an–an avenue walker who tries to get money, and then you want to take me to a meal. How do I know what to expect from you?"

He wanted to laugh but didn't dare. "Streetwalker," he murmured.

"What?"

"Streetwalker, not avenue walker."

"Very well. Streetwalker." She leaned over and prodded his chest with her small finger. "I am not a woman who looks to men for money. If I wanted that, I could have done that in Russia. I want what is best for Irina, only for Irina."

She was a good mother; he had to give her that. Those sapphire eyes bore into his with an intensity that made him flinch. He didn't think he'd ever met a woman who cared more fiercely for her child. A pang of regret smote him. He'd handled this all wrong. She wasn't what she seemed at first.

He cleared his throat. "You're right. I'm a heel."

Her expression of outrage changed to confusion. "Heel? You are not a shoe."

He laughed. "Heel. As in only worthy to be walked on. I misjudged you, Tatiana. You're a good woman, a good mother. Please, accept my apology. Let's start over."

Suspicion still shone in her eyes. "That is what you said this morning. But you still order me to do what you say as you speak to a child."

He nodded meekly. "I know. I haven't had much experience with women. That's why Mike thought he had to find me a wife."

Her eyes widened. "You could marry anyone you want."

"Because of my money," he said.

She shook her head. "You are very handsome. Surely, you know this."

A strange sensation spread through his chest. She thought he was attractive. He could read the sincerity in her eyes. He'd met so many women who were interested in him because of his money. It had made him leery of entanglements. He didn't know what was happening to him, and he wasn't entirely sure he liked it.

He looked away from her gaze. "Does that mean you accept my apology?"

She laughed. "Heel." She said the word as if trying it on for size. "I accept. But if you act like this again, I shall not be so kind next time."

He chuckled. "I accept your conditions."

They reached the edge of Wabash, and he turned onto Vernon Street and drove across the bridge. "How about some soup and espresso for lunch?"

"I love espresso," she said. "The restaurant where I work in Russia had only me make it."

He drove around the city block so he could park on Wabash Street facing south. The old First National Bank was now city hall, and he parked along the street in front of it. Hopping out, he unbuckled Irina and hoisted her into his arms. The feel of her small arms around his neck brought a lump to his throat.

Tatiana held out her arms for her daughter, but Irina hid her face in his neck. "I stay with Daddy," she said.

Tatiana's arms dropped, and she smiled ruefully. "She doesn't usually like men."

The lump in his throat grew bigger. What was happening to him? The shell he'd built around his heart seemed to be melting. He led the way to Metro Espresso. Pushing open the door, he breathed in the rich coffee aroma.

Steven, the owner, waved to them as Gabe led the way to a back table. Steven finished waiting on another customer then came to the table. "What'll it be today, Gabe?"

"My usual and a cup of Lisa's chicken soup. What do you want, Tatiana?"

"Soup for me and Irina. Do you have milk?"

Steven nodded.

"Milk for Irina and a mocha for me," she said.

Steven returned to the counter to prepare their order.

"I like this place," she said. "The woodwork is lovely, and it even has a tin ceiling."

Gabe nodded. "It's my favorite place. They have the best espresso I've ever had."

Steven brought their order, and Tatiana nodded after her first sip. "You are right, Gabe. This is wonderful." She sipped it slowly and closed her eyes, an ecstatic expression on her face.

He watched Tatiana a moment, then turned his attention to his soup. Irina was nodding sleepily by the time he left his money on the table and carried her back into the February cold.

"May we walk around the town instead of drive? Wabash is merely a village," Tatiana said. "I enjoy the fresh air."

He nodded. "I have something I need to do here anyway." He led the way around the corner onto Market Street. She stopped and stared into Billings Flower and Gifts. The window display was lavish, and he pushed open the door and motioned for her to enter. Her eyes lit up, and she eagerly went inside.

The aroma of candles and potpourri lingered in the air. Tatiana dawdled over a collection of china dolls, and Irina fingered a Boyd bear longingly. Gabe picked it up. "Would you like this, sugar?"

Irina's eyes widened, and she put her thumb in her mouth. Her gaze shot to her mother's as if to ask for permission, but Tatiana was still admiring the china dolls.

Irina nodded slowly. He handed it to her. Her little arms crept around it, and she hugged it close. Running to her mother, she showed it to her.

Tatiana searched his gaze with her sapphire one. "You must not spoil her," she said softly.

"I want to." He discovered he would like to spoil Irina's mother as well. Picking up a doll lavishly dressed in blue silk, he carried it toward the checkout.

"Wait, you cannot." Tatiana's voice was bewildered.

"It's a peace offering," he said. "Please don't spoil my enjoyment."

She bit her lip, obviously torn by his plea. Inclining her head, she sighed. "As you wish. I shall prepare you a wonderful supper to say thank you. May I buy the ingredients I need?"

"We'll stop at the grocery on the way home." He paid for the bear and the doll, then led them next door to The Francis Shoppe. When she saw he meant to enter, Tatiana held up a hand in protest. "No—no more gifts."

"This is a necessity," he said. "I brought you to town to buy you and Irina new coats. We'll buy yours first, then go across town to get Irina's."

She stiffened her shoulders. "Our coats are fine. If you are ashamed of us, we can go home now."

"I'm not ashamed of you. But it's cold, and I would feel better if Irina had a warmer one. You, too." His mention of her daughter had the desired effect, for her glare softened.

"For Irina then. I do not need one."

He reached out and touched her arm. "I need to ask a favor."

She scowled. "I want no coat."

"That's not the favor." He pulled them nearer the door and out of the wind. "Mother has been planning a dinner party for her seventieth birthday for months. It's this Saturday. Would you be interested in working for us and preparing the food for the party? It would mean so much to Mother."

Her gaze searched his, and she seemed to see his sincerity. "I would be honored with this trust."

He smiled cajolingly. "So, you see, the coat could be just an advance on your salary."

Tatiana shook her head. "I would not spend my money so foolishly when Irina needs new clothes. Let us go to this place where we can find her a coat, and you may advance me money there for her."

So much for that idea. He knew when he was licked. "Let me show you the downtown first. All two blocks square of it." Wabash still held its Victorian flavor with its tall storefronts. The Eagles Theater was one of the oldest. He would have to take her to a movie sometime. At the errant thought, he suppressed a sigh. His thoughts refused to stay corralled.

Irina cried out and pointed to a kitten in the window of J & K Pet Store, but Tatiana refused to go in. "You do not need a kitten," she said firmly. "You have a new bear."

Irina started to cry, and she rubbed her eyes tiredly. Gabe knelt beside her. "What's your bear's name?" he asked.

Her tears stopped, and she considered his question carefully. "Pooh," she said.

"He's not yellow."

"Pooh," she repeated.

"Okay, Pooh it is." He held out his arms. "You're tired.

Want me to carry you?"

She nodded, and he lifted her into his arms. "Let's go buy you a new coat. Your mommy can't complain about that." He turned to smile at Tatiana, but his grin faltered at the tears in her eyes.

"What did I say this time?" he asked.

"Nothing," she whispered. "There are so many things Irina will never have. Never, never." She turned and walked back to the Jeep, her erect carriage belying the pain he'd just seen in her eyes.

His emotions in turmoil, he followed her to the Jeep. Irina was asleep by the time he fastened her into the seat belt. The air was stiff with Tatiana's misery as he pulled out, then turned to go north to the children's shop. "I'm sorry," he said after a long pause. "Sorry for the pain you've had in your life, sorry you have no husband to share the burden with, sorry Irina has no father. But your Heavenly Father is always there for you."

Tatiana's eyes narrowed. "Do not speak to me of a Heavenly Father," she said with an angry toss of her head. "Irina lost her father because he was a Christian. Sergio, he think his faith is worth more than his child and his wife. Because of this religion, Irina and I live on bread and milk. I want nothing to do with your Jesus."

Pain squeezed his heart. He had begun to think he might keep an open mind about a relationship with Tatiana. But that was impossible if she wasn't a believer. "I'm sorry to hear that," he said quietly. "Knowing Jesus is the only thing that has given me peace in many circumstances of my life." His emotions rolled from the blow. Until that moment, he hadn't realized how much he was attracted to her.

Tears squeezed from her lids. "What trouble could you have had, Mr. Salinger? You, who live in such luxury? Do you know what it is like to go to bed and hear your child whimper with hunger? What it is like to worry that you and your daughter will be thrown onto the street because you have no money to pay rent?"

"No," he said quietly, "but I know what it's like to see my father die a lingering death from cancer. I know what it's like to lose a sister who went swimming one day and didn't come back. I know about loss, Tatiana. Money doesn't make me exempt from pain."

Shame darkened her eyes, and she looked away. "You are right. I am sorry," she whispered.

He nodded. "Here we are." He stopped the car outside Jack in the Box, a children's clothing store. Unfastening the seat belt, he lifted the sleeping little girl into his arms and carried her inside. She didn't stir. He could sense Tatiana's remorse over her harsh words, but that didn't change the fact that she wasn't a Christian.

They shopped in silence. Tatiana let him buy Irina a new coat, navy blue with gold buttons, and a blue and yellow Pooh scarf, as well as five sturdy play outfits and two dresses. The light in her eyes as they added the gaily colored clothing to their cart lifted his spirits. The shop also had a car seat, so he bought that, too. He handed Irina to Tatiana while he went to the Jeep and fastened it in place.

"Now, let's get those groceries and head for home," he said after putting the sleeping child into the seat.

Tatiana nodded and climbed into the Jeep. He drove south to Bechtol's Grocery. Again, he unfastened Irina and carried her inside. This child stuff was wearing. Fasten her in;

unfasten her. No wonder he saw mothers worn out when shopping with their children. Before today, he'd had no idea it was so hard. But it was also fun in some strange way.

Irina was awake by the time they got inside the store. Her eyes were as big as her mother's as they started down the aisles.

"Never have I seen so much choice," Tatiana marveled. "And so inexpensive." She selected beef, vegetables, pasta, constantly checking prices. "I am ready."

He fished out his wallet, and she held up her hand. "You said I might buy the food."

"I didn't say you could buy it. I said we'd stop at the store." He shuddered to think how little money there was in her battered purse.

"No, I insist." She compressed her lips and marched toward the checkout line.

He sighed and followed her. That pride of hers was unrelenting. But he admired her independence. Most women would have taken anything he offered.

She carefully counted out her money and handed it to the clerk. Her smile was joyful as she carried Irina back to the car. "Wait until you taste the supper I shall prepare for you. Will Mike and your mother be there?"

"Yes," he assured her. "Especially when they hear you're cooking a Russian meal. Do I get a hint of what you're fixing?"

"*Nyet*. You must be surprised with the rest." She clapped her hands joyfully. "I love to cook when I can find such good ingredients. I must thank your mother for allowing me this chance to repay her kindness."

"We are the ones who are grateful. I would have hated to

cancel the party. Mother's old friend, Major MacGregor, is in town." He dropped his voice to a whisper. "I've had hopes they might make a match one of these days, but Mother is so stubborn and won't see him unless it's in a group. I know he has loved her for years."

Tatiana turned her wide eyes on him. "Not many sons would feel this way. Many would be jealous."

He shrugged. "I just want her to be happy. And, besides, maybe if she has a husband, she won't be moaning so much about grandchildren."

The corners of Tatiana's mouth quirked up. "It is a hard life for you," she said cheekily.

He laughed and parked the Jeep outside the house. "You carry Irina; I'll get the groceries," he said. "You don't know what you're in for with my mother. She'll find you a husband, I can guarantee it."

"But it won't be you," Tatiana said flatly.

His smile faded. "No, it won't be me."

six

Tatiana put the china doll on her dresser and smiled into its painted face. She had always wanted a doll like this, but the closest she'd ever come was a cloth doll her mother had made for her when she was two. Gabe was a kind and generous man. Why did he refuse to consider the idea of a life with her? She was no great beauty, but she was fairly attractive. Maybe he didn't like blonds. Sighing, she pulled her hair back and went to prepare supper. On the way, she peeked into Irina's room and saw her playing happily with her new bear.

Gabe had put the groceries away by the time she got there. Pouring a cup of coffee, he didn't notice her in the doorway. She was able to stand and just look at him. Why did he draw her the way he did? Mike looked just like him, same gray eyes that reminded her of the sea on a stormy day, same broad shoulders and slender fingers, same square jaw. But being around Mike didn't make her catch her breath; he didn't cause her heart to pound the way it was right now. She shook her head slightly to clear it, and Gabe turned.

He eyed her scraped-back hair but didn't remark on it. "I suppose you're going to tell me I have to leave the kitchen so you can cook," he said.

The wistful tone in his voice tugged at her heartstrings. He was like a little boy who was told to leave the swing set and go to bed. Smiling, she shook her head. "If you really wish to help, I will let you."

His eyes brightened, and he took a swig of coffee. "I love to cook, but Martha never lets me. She grew up in the days when it was shameful for a man to be in the kitchen. This is my favorite room, but she never lets me stay long. Want me to fix the salad?"

Her smile widened at the eagerness in his voice. "One does not sharpen the axes *after* the right time. First, you may cut up chunks of chicken breast for me." She went to the refrigerator and pulled out the ingredients. "I will chop the vegetables."

Gabe rummaged until he found a couple of chopping boards and knives. They worked in companionable silence for several minutes. Sergio had never been interested in cooking, and Tatiana found it refreshing to have a man in her kitchen.

"What is this bread you made this morning?" Gabe asked. "I've been wanting a piece since I saw it."

"Russian black bread," she said. "Full of flavor and chewy. I think you will like it."

"Sounds good." He stared at it longingly, then turned back to his chicken. "I think that's done. What now?"

"Find me a pot to cook the stew in." She used the knife to move the vegetables together on the chopping board. "Have you a—a thing that squeezes the juice from these?" She couldn't think of the English word for the tool or the vegetable.

"Garlic press," he said. "I'm sure we do." He sifted through the drawers and found what she needed. Hovering at her elbow, he watched her press the garlic and combine the ingredients in the pot. "Don't you think I deserve to know what this is we're cooking?"

She found his nearness distracting. What would it be like to have such a strong and kind man as a husband? Suppressing a sigh, she smiled. "It is called Midnight Chicken. You may put many different things in it, depending on what is in your refrigerator at midnight when unexpected guests stop in."

He chuckled and moved closer to the stove, which meant he also moved closer to her. Her mouth went dry, and she longed to lean back against his broad chest. Biting her lip, she moved away a few inches.

He took the spoon and stirred the stew. "What else?"

"This is put over rice noodles. We must prepare a salad, and maybe an Armenian cheese roll for an appetizer. I will prepare Russian Pryaniks—maybe you call them honey cakes—for dessert and also lemon tarts with blueberry sauce."

Gabe stopped stirring a moment. "You must be quite a cook," he said softly.

The warmth in his gaze disconcerted her a moment. "It is something I enjoy." She could see the admiration in his eyes. Why would he not admit it? It was beyond her understanding.

Gabe seemed to realize how close he was, for his gray eyes lost their light, and he moved away. His tone became brisk and impersonal. "You ready for that salad now?"

"Not yet. It must be fresh. Maybe you could check on Irina while I make the dessert?"

"Maybe that would be best," he said gravely.

With an aching heart, she watched him leave. If she felt

like this after only two days, what would the rest of the ninety days bring? Likely heartache. The thought didn't frighten her. She'd faced heartache before. If it came, it came. At least Irina was safe and warm for now.

&

Grace returned around four o'clock. Her face lined with strain, she dropped into the chair at the kitchen table and kicked off her shoes. "Poor Martha. She will be laid up for at least two or three months. I shall have to try to find some help from the temp agency in town." Looking around the kitchen, she smiled. "But it looks like you have everything under control for now. You didn't have to cook supper. We could have gone out."

"I did not want you to have to go to the village when you would be tired," Tatiana said, pouring Grace a cup of coffee. "Besides, I love to cook." She sat beside her at the table and propped her chin in her hand. "I would like to work for you while I am here, if you would allow it."

"You mean, take Martha's place?" Gabe's mother's gray look lightened a bit. "Why didn't I think of that? Are you sure you're up to it? This is a large house."

"I am stronger than I look," Tatiana said. "Since I must return to Russia, it would give me the opportunity to earn some money before I go."

Grace shook her head. "We'll find you a husband. You'll see. But that's a splendid idea about acting as our housekeeper and cook. You'll stay in your present rooms, of course. That will be much more convenient than having you across the estate in the guest cottage. Besides, it will give Gabe a chance to get to know you better."

Heat spread up Tatiana's cheeks. "You would wish this?"

Grace was silent a moment. "I already like you, Tatiana. But I don't know you well enough yet to determine if you are the one God has chosen for my Gabe. We haven't talked about your faith or anything else important. But I know we all must learn more about one another. Only time will tell about any future relationship."

Tatiana dropped her head so Grace would not see how her words had affected her. What should she say about faith? She couldn't lie. Could these people really take it so seriously? "I do not think Gabe wishes to get to know me better," she said.

Grace clicked her tongue. "How would he know that yet? All we can do is pray that God would show us the right thing to do as we learn about one another."

God again. Why did the subject seem to follow her everywhere she went, like a—a stray cat? Tatiana clenched her hands in the folds of her skirt. A tide of rebellion choked her. Did all Christians try to force their views on everyone? She was sick of it. Why couldn't they leave her alone? She just wanted a place for Irina and herself, not a sermon.

Grace took her silence for agreement. Patting her hand, she rose. "I think I'll shower before supper. Is there anything I can do to help?"

"Gabe already helped me. Everything is in order. The stew will be ready around six. Is that acceptable?"

"Wonderful." She paused at the doorway. "How is our girl today? You are very fortunate to have such a wonderful daughter. I shall enjoy having her around. Tomorrow I would like to take you both shopping. My treat, of course."

"I beat you to it, Mother." Gabe dropped a kiss on his

mother's cheek, then strode into the kitchen and sat on a bar stool at the island.

Grace cast a bewildered look from Gabe to Tatiana. "You went shopping? You?"

He shrugged. "I do occasionally have to go in a store, you know."

"Yes, but you hate shopping."

"I found it rather enjoyable today," he said.

Tatiana was conscious of his thoughtful gaze and hurriedly went to the stove to stir the stew. "He purchased for Irina some clothing and a coat as well as a bear. For me, he also purchased a doll." She turned and smiled. No one had ever bought her such a frivolous present before. She found she liked being frivolous.

Gabe flushed at her smile of gratitude. "Maybe Tatiana will let you buy her a coat. She wouldn't let me."

"I see," Grace said faintly. "Well, I shall see what I can do tomorrow. We'll stop and check on Martha, then I'll take you to lunch and to Fort Wayne to shop."

"Thank you," Tatiana said. "I would love to spend the time with you." And it would get her away from Gabe. She needed to catch her breath a bit and marshal her defenses against his magnetism.

The front door slammed. "Mike is home," Grace said. "I must speak with him a moment." She gave Gabe and Tatiana a slight wave and hurried from the room.

"That smells good," Gabe said. "Irina was asking for you. I'll watch it if you want to see what she needs. I think she just wanted to be reassured you were close by."

Tatiana nodded and untied her apron. "It is still all new and strange to her. And to me," she added. She was glad to escape his presence. He disturbed her in ways she couldn't put her finger on. Though she knew he and Mike were identical twins, she had no trouble now telling the two of them apart.

Irina sat in a corner of the large nursery with blocks spread around her. She'd built a house for her bear and was busy peering inside. She squealed when she saw her mother and ran to hug her. Tatiana spent a few minutes with her, then started back to the kitchen. She heard Gabe singing. In a deep baritone voice, he sang something about walking by faith and not by sight.

A longing as sharp as a cramp gripped Tatiana. Where did these Christians get their blind faith? How could they ignore the bad things that happened around them and to them and still worship this Jesus? She hadn't understood it when Sergio was alive, and she didn't understand it now. But to have such confidence in the future was very alluring. Her heart was in a quandary of fear and trepidation about what would happen to her and Irina. To be able to rest in someone else's strength would be wonderful.

The sting of tears awoke her from her reverie. Shaking her head, she continued on to the kitchen. She wouldn't be that weak. Standing on her own might be hard, but it was something she was proud of. She shivered at the thought of turning that burden over to someone else. It was hers, and she would bear it.

After supper, she put the dishes in the dishwasher while Gabe took Irina to the family room and put on a video for her to watch. It was something called "Adventures in Odyssey." Tatiana wanted to see it herself, so she hurried through her chores in the kitchen. Once the dishes were cleared, she prepared batter for *blinis* for breakfast and put it on the stove to rise.

Irina was giggling as Tatiana walked into the family room. She was curled up in the crook of Gabe's arm with her thumb in her mouth.

"Irina!" Tatiana said sharply. "Your thumb." She frowned and shook her head.

Irina's smile faded, and she reluctantly pulled her hand away from her mouth.

Gabe's lips tightened, but he didn't say anything. Tatiana sat in the rocker and watched the rest of the video. She laughed with the rest of them, and she found her spirits lighter as she carried Irina upstairs and put her to bed. It was nice to feel part of a family, even if it was only temporary.

The next day sped by. She asked Grace to take her to a place that sold used clothing and found several suitable dresses for herself as well as a warm coat. Grace insisted on buying her a new dress as well, but she didn't like the feeling of accepting charity. When the older woman seemed to receive so much joy from it, Tatiana didn't have the heart to refuse.

The next few days fell into a pleasant pattern. She cooked, cleaned, washed, and nurtured the family. When they visited the hospital, even grumpy Martha seemed to relax when she heard the glowing reports from the rest of the family about how well Tatiana was caring for them all.

Tatiana took special care to plan the party menu. She took her plans to Grace.

"Goodness, Tatiana, this is much more elaborate than even Martha would have done. You have four appetizers alone! Are you sure you want to go to all that trouble?"

"The cooking, I enjoy," she said. "The menu, it is adequate?"

"More than adequate. My guests will try to steal you away from me." Grace laughed and handed the menu to her.

Tatiana smiled and went back to the kitchen. If only a male guest would show some interest. Though it was going to be hard to distract herself from Gabe. He occupied her thoughts way too often.

❧

Saturday night, Tatiana washed the last counter and turned out the kitchen light. The dinner had gone splendidly. The guests had raved about the food, and Grace took pride in showing off Tatiana. Grace's thoughtfulness had warmed Tatiana's heart. Unfortunately, there had been no men young enough to be interested in a wife. The only unmarried man had been Major MacGregor, and his gaze had never left Grace's face. Tatiana smiled at the memory.

Grace insisted she take Sundays off, but she had prepared casseroles for their meals and would just have to slip them in the oven. The thought of a day of rest was appealing. She had felt she was on trial this entire week, though she knew none of the Salingers felt that way.

She went to the door leading to the family room. Gabe had his feet on the coffee table while Mike lounged on the love seat with his feet propped on the back of it. The careless posture of these Americans was atrocious. Unconsciously, Tatiana straightened her own shoulders.

Grace saw her in the doorway and smiled. "There you are. I was about to come looking for you. We leave for church about nine. Gabe will pull the Jeep up front and honk. Wear your new dress. I'm eager to see you in it."

Tatiana gulped. How did she tell the older woman she had sworn never to set foot in a church? She caught Gabe's amused glance. He knew her feelings and was enjoying her discomfiture; she could see it on his smug face. She opened her mouth to refuse, but the words stuck in her throat. How could she disappoint Grace when she had done so much for her? It would be churlish.

She narrowed her eyes at Gabe. "Very well," she said quietly. Astonishment raced over Gabe's features, but he quickly hid it. He evidently caught her warning, for he didn't say anything. And why would he? He was a Christian, too. They all thought she needed to be converted, whatever that meant. Even Sergio had prayed for her, much to her chagrin. But her parents hadn't raised her to accept such fairy tales.

She escaped as quickly as she could. The thought of sitting in a stuffy church all morning didn't appeal at all to her. She'd attended the state church once when she was a teenager, but the stained glass and the rituals were intimidating. Everyone had known the moves but her, and she was in no hurry to feel so foolish again.

She sighed and peeked in on Irina. She had taken to this new life like she was born to it. Her curls lay on the pillow around her small head, and she slept peacefully. Tatiana closed her bedroom door and went to run her bath. Tomorrow would be an ordeal.

*

She awoke feeling as though she'd barely slept. Sunshine streamed in the window, and she could hear the sounds of showers running. Grace had her usual radio station playing. *WFRN, your friend,* it often said. In spite of herself, Tatiana had listened to it over the past few days and some part of her was drawn to the uplifting music and the family values it spoke of.

A heavy ball of dread formed in her stomach as she dressed in her new dress. The periwinkle sheath skimmed her figure and fell to her calves. Looking in the mirror, she thought she wouldn't disgrace the Salingers today. She caught the top of her shoulder-length hair back in a bow and then went to get Irina ready.

Gabe's voice echoed from Irina's room. Tatiana stood in the doorway and listened to him talk to her daughter. "You have really pretty hair."

Peeking inside, she saw him brushing Irina's curls. She was already dressed in her new red dress. Her hands clasped in her lap, she sat with her head still, which was more than she usually did for her mother.

Gabe looked up and saw her in the door, and his eyes widened. "Wow, you look—you look lovely." He looked away quickly. "Mother got Irina dressed and told me to brush her hair. I've probably made a mess of it."

He was actually doing a pretty good job, but she wasn't about to tell him. "You think we are not ready in time? Your mother, I promised. I would not go back on my word."

"Caught you, didn't she?"

She scowled at him. "Only because I love your mother. I will not enjoy it."

"Don't make your mind up before you get there. You might like it."

"Faith is too dangerous," she said. "I would not wish Irina to be harmed."

"You're in America now," he said. "It's not dangerous here. Yet."

Yet. What did he mean? She stared up at him, then mentally shrugged. Who knew what these Christians meant by anything they said? They spoke in riddles and language she didn't understand. "Her hair I will finish." She held out her hand for the brush.

He gave her a cheeky grin and handed it to her. "Was I doing that bad of a job?"

She didn't answer but simply pulled the top of Irina's hair back and secured it with a bow.

"Here's her shoes." He handed her a pair of patent leather shoes Grace had bought.

She took them and slipped them on Irina's feet. "Ready, my lamb?"

"Can I take Pooh?" Irina picked up her bear and clutched it close to her chest.

"Sure," Gabe said before Tatiana could refuse.

Tatiana stared at him doubtfully. "You are certain?" In the church of her memory, such frivolity would be frowned upon.

"Some parents even take coloring books and crayons to keep the kids busy. But we have Sunday school and junior church, so she'll have fun."

The words were incomprehensible to Tatiana. School? What did they teach? She was almost afraid to find out. But surely one lesson wouldn't harm Irina. She would try to find an excuse from now on. She took Irina's hand and turned to Gabe. "We are ready."

"We usually stop for breakfast. I'll get Mother."

"Mike is not going?" How did he get out of it?

"He might show up for church." Gabe's eyes darkened.

So Mike wasn't a Christian. Could that be the difference

she sensed in the two men? Could that be the strength and reliability she sensed in Gabe? The thought was a bit disconcerting. She and Irina followed Gabe down the hall.

Grace came from the living room and smiled when she saw them. "You both look darling."

"What about me?" Gabe asked in an injured tone.

"You, too, Son. But just look at our girls. Irina's curls are so lovely." She touched the little girl's head.

But Gabe wasn't looking at Irina, and the expression in his gaze sent Tatiana's heart racing. She looked away. Going to the closet, she got out her coat and slipped it on, then put Irina's on her.

Gabe picked up Irina, and she wrapped one arm around his neck while the other still clutched her bear. She pressed her cheek against his. The sight gave Tatiana a strange pang. Turning away, she went to the door and held it open for him to carry Irina to the car. Grace bustled along behind him.

They rode to town in silence, but it wasn't the uncomfortable sort that left her searching for something to say. It was companionable, as though they'd done this trip many times. After stopping at Burger King for a quick breakfast, Gabe turned back onto Indiana 15 and seemed to be leaving town again.

"Your church, it is in the countryside?" How strange for a large, spired building to be built where no one could admire it.

Gabe nodded. He didn't seem inclined to explain, so Tatiana lapsed into silence again herself. They drove for several minutes, then turned onto a country road. Moments later, they turned into the parking lot of a brown-and-tan building with a small white steeple. The church building was one story and unassuming. New Life Bible Church, the sign said. This was a church? Her husband had told her the church he attended in St. Petersburg was in a small building, but she had thought it was his way of dismissing her fears of the usual grand edifice.

The tension in her shoulder muscles eased, and she smiled at Irina as she unbuckled her car seat. Gabe lifted the little girl out and carried her through the snow to the church. Several smiling people, men and women alike, stood near the entrance. They shook her hand, exclaimed over Irina, and welcomed her to the service. Gabe took Irina away to the place he called Sunday school, and Tatiana felt strangely bereft at his absence.

She wanted to sit in the back where no one would notice her, but Grace led her to a cushioned pew near the front of the church. In spite of its unassuming exterior, the inside of the church was gracious with warm oak trim and accents as well as a beautiful wooden cross at the front. Before she had finished looking around, Gabe joined them in the pew.

"Irina, she is happy?" Tatiana curled her fingers into the palms of her hands. She didn't know why she felt so anxious.

Gabe smiled reassuringly. "She's fine. Playing with the other kids and showing off her Pooh."

Tatiana let out her breath and turned her gaze from Gabe's probing eyes. She focused on the front of the church again. The pastor, Steve Parks, stepped to the front and welcomed the people to church. An attractive man in his forties with penetrating blue eyes and black hair shot through with silver, he mentioned Tatiana by name, and she wanted to shrink back into the pew.

Next they sang songs. Grace held a songbook for her to look at the words. One song in particular tugged at Tatiana's heartstrings in a way that made her want to flee the church.

Be still, my soul; the Lord is on thy side. Bear patiently the cross of grief or pain.

She had never felt the sense of knowing someone powerful was on her side. A film of tears obscured her vision, and she blinked furiously. She mustn't cry. Gabe and Grace would think the service was affecting her. Digging her nails into the palm of her hands, she managed to get hold of her emotions. She would get through this service and find a way to get out of ever coming again.

seven

Gabe sighed and closed his desk drawer. Customers changing their minds, problems with contractors. . .had this week finally ended? He grabbed his coat and headed toward the door.

"Hey, wait a sec, Gabe." Mike hurried toward him with another man in tow. "I wanted you to meet Jason Bechtol before I brought him home with me. He's with Marlow and Truly, the new contractors in Fort Wayne."

The man reminded Gabe of a basset hound with the bags under his eyes and the morose air that seemed to hang around him. His brown eyes and light brown hair all blended together with his sallow skin, and he seemed colorless. The name was familiar, though.

"Pleased to meet you." Gabe shook his hand, releasing it as quickly as politeness would allow. He hated a limp-wrist handshake.

"Jason is interested in meeting Tatiana." The smile Mike flashed was full of pride and self-congratulation.

The muscle in Gabe's jaw twitched. Did Mike seriously believe this wimpish guy would make a suitable mate for Tatiana? He controlled his temper with an effort. "I see."

"My divorce was final six months ago, and I thought I might start looking around," Jason said. His voice was as colorless as his appearance.

Looking around. Gabe wanted to tell him Tatiana wasn't

a car, but he refrained. The man was a colleague, after all. "Why were you divorced?"

Mike's eyes widened at the impertinent question. He shot Gabe a pleading glance and shook his head slightly. Gabe ignored him. He didn't want Tatiana marrying some guy who would beat her or something.

A hint of red tinged Jason's colorless cheeks. "Uh, well. . ." His voice trailed off, and he looked away. Clearing his throat, he continued. "We grew apart. You know how things are."

In that moment, Gabe realized why the man's name was familiar. It had been all over the papers. He'd been caught with another woman, and his wife had come after him and the girlfriend with a gun. The ex was in jail, and the girlfriend had dumped him and married some tycoon from Chicago.

He stared from Jason to Mike. Mike colored at the accusation Gabe didn't try to hide. He shuffled his feet and looked away. "Uh, we'd better get going, Gabe. I told Mother we'd be there in fifteen minutes."

He had no choice but to follow his brother and Jason to the exit. The March wind whipped down Canal Street, and he poked his icy fingers under his coat. Waving Mike on, he stopped at Metro Espresso for a cappuccino. He needed a minute to himself. This needed delicate handling. Tatiana would be sure to think he was interfering if he threw the guy out of the house.

Sipping the hot drink, he drove slowly toward home. The lights blazed from the house as he turned in the driveway. His heart sped up a bit at the thought of seeing Tatiana. These past few days he'd looked forward to coming home as never before, and he didn't like the realization. It really would be best to find her a husband and get her gone from the house, but his heart ached at the thought.

The welcoming scent of some kind of beef dish teased his nose when he shut the door behind him. Every night there had been some new culinary delight to try, and it smelled like tonight was no exception. His mouth watered at the aroma. He hung his coat in the closet and walked toward the kitchen. The murmur of voices grew as he neared the welcome warmth of the kitchen.

Tatiana stood with flour on her hands as well as a dusting on her nose. She was smiling up at Jason, and Gabe didn't like the expression on her face. She looked—interested. He cleared his throat, and she turned toward the door. Her smile faded when she saw Gabe, and she stepped back and wiped her floury hands on her apron.

"The meal, it will be ready soon," she said.

He stepped further into the kitchen. "Smells good. What is it?"

"Beef Stroganoff." She leaned over a skillet and stirred the bubbling concoction. A flush tinged her cheeks, and she avoided his gaze.

"Tatiana is quite the cook," Mike said. He enumerated her good qualities the way an owner listed a car's attributes. Gabe expected the sticker price to come next. "The house is always spotless, and you should taste those *blini* things she makes for breakfast. She made that dried flower arrangement in the entry—you had to have noticed it."

The color on Tatiana's face deepened, and she stirred the skillet more briskly. "It was nothing. Anyone could do it."

Mike laughed. "I couldn't." He took Jason's arm and

tugged him toward the door. "We've got a few minutes before dinner. Let me show you the wallpaper she put up in the laundry room."

Jason was staring at Tatiana with a besotted expression on his hangdog face, and Gabe clenched his hands into fists. He couldn't be—jealous—could he? Gritting his teeth, he held his tongue until Mike succeeded in dragging Jason away to see evidences of Tatiana's qualifications to be the perfect wife. His brother had no sense. He'd always known it, but this was indisputable proof.

"Where's Irina?"

"Napping. She should awaken at any moment."

She stirred the sauce so industriously, it was a wonder she hadn't worn a hole through the bottom of the skillet. Her blond hair was twisted onto the top of her head, but fine tendrils caressed her cheeks and the back of her neck. She looked altogether lovely and competent at the same time. Gabe resisted the impulse to press his lips against the nape of her slim neck. What was happening to him? He'd never felt this way about a woman before.

"I'm sorry you had to put up with Mike's matchmaking." He poured a cup of coffee from the coffee butler and took a gulp.

Tatiana raised her eyebrows. "You would begrudge the help Mike offers to me? I must find a husband. You know this."

"Maybe we could get you a visa to stay." He'd been thinking about it this week. Surely, it shouldn't be that difficult.

She laughed. "I have no skills that are in demand by your economy, no computer training, no professional school. In Russia I am a cook. I do not think there is a need for such as I. And even if you arranged a visa, how would we live?"

"I could loan you the money to open a Russian café. You could serve the same kinds of things you've been feeding us." He raised his voice a bit in his eagerness to convince her.

The flush on her cheeks deepened as she stared at him. "Why would you do this? You do not wish to marry me, so why do you care what happens to us?"

"I don't want to see you go back to Russia. Any Christian would feel the same," he said stiffly.

She nodded slowly. "If you could do this, I would be grateful."

"You would consider staying even without a husband?" Joy bubbled up inside him. He didn't stop to evaluate why he felt such elation.

Tatiana shrugged. "I do not think I will be allowed, but you can try."

Gabe felt as if a huge stone had been rolled off his shoulders. Surely, he could arrange it. Then there would be time to win her to the Lord as well. He didn't dare poke too closely into his reasons for his relief. "Can I wake up Irina?"

"I think I hear her now."

He turned at the patter of small feet. Irina burst into the kitchen, her corkscrew curls askew and the flush of sleep still on her cheeks. She rushed to him, and he lifted her into his arms. Wrapping her arms around his neck, she snuggled against his chest.

"I am hungry, *Mat*." Irina rubbed her eyes.

Gabe grinned. "Me, too."

"Tell Mike and Jason to wash for dinner. I will put it on the table. Your mother is in the living room." Tatiana turned away and began to rinse the noodles in the sink.

Jason. He still had to get rid of him. His high spirits faded. Grimly, he set Irina on the floor and went to find Jason and Mike. They were just coming down the stairs, and he stood waiting for them at the bottom.

"Dinner's ready." Gabe didn't like the self-satisfied smirk on Jason's face. A philanderer like him didn't deserve a woman like Tatiana.

Mike clapped Jason on the back. "Now you get to taste some of Tatiana's fabulous cooking." He patted his stomach. "I've gained five pounds in the ten days she's been here."

"Could I speak to you a moment, Mike?" Gabe asked. "In private."

Mike's eyes widened, and he shrugged. "Sure." He pointed Jason toward the dining room door. "I'll meet you in the dining room."

Gabe waited until Jason left. "Have you lost your mind? That man cheated on his wife and was nearly killed for it. It was all over the papers. Is that the kind of husband you want for Tatiana? What if his crackpot wife comes after her next?"

Mike had the grace to look shamefaced. "He was the best I've been able to do," he said. "I've mentioned her to everyone else, and no one else wanted to meet her."

"No one would be better than a man like that. You have to get rid of him."

Mike studied him a moment. "You're jealous," he said incredulously. A jubilant grin stretched across his face. "I can see it all over you!" He rubbed his hands together. "There's going to be a wedding, after all."

Gabe took several deep, calming breaths. *Control; don't*

lose control. "You know I can't marry her," he said. "She isn't a Christian."

Mike's grin faded. "Just because she's not a Christian," he said in disgust. "Give her time, and she'll be just as much a fanatic as you. You could marry her and change her later."

"You know I can't do that. The Bible says not to be unequally yoked together."

Mike gave a snort of disgust. "You're not denying you're jealous, though."

Gabe winced at the smugness of Mike's tone. "Of course, I'm not jealous." His words sounded weak, even to himself.

"It's just another instance of that famous self-control of yours," Mike said. "You would never be able to admit that, just maybe, you even *have* feelings."

"And you're still trying to pin the blame for this situation on me instead of yourself," Gabe shot back. "You're the one who brought her here."

"You'll never let me forget that lapse of judgment, will you?" Mike stalked toward the door, then gave one last parting shot. "You might let the best thing that ever happened to you slip right through your fingers." The pictures on the walls shook with the force of the door's slam.

Gabe released the breath he'd been holding. That had not gone well. Why did his life seem to be unraveling right before his eyes? He rubbed his burning eyes. The best thing to do was to get her permission to stay and then get her out of the house, out of temptation's way. She drew him way too much.

Tatiana was laughing at a joke Jason had just told when Gabe entered the dining room. Her laughter died when he walked in, and she put the last bowl of food on the table and slid into her seat. Gabe's jaw tightened at the glance Jason shot him, full of insolence and challenge. Maybe opposition wasn't the best way to get rid of him. He was obviously out to score points.

Gabe found it difficult to keep from staring at Tatiana over dinner. She looked especially lovely in a coral sweater and black slacks. Her dark blue eyes shone at the attention Jason was giving her. It was all Gabe could do to choke down his food. Everyone else remarked about the delicious Stroganoff, but he could have been eating sand and not known the difference.

"*Mat,* can I watch the Barney video?" Irina asked as Tatiana began to clear the dinner dishes away.

"After your bath," Tatiana said.

"We'll have dessert in the family room," Grace said. "I'll entertain the men until you join us." Grace led Mike and Jason out the door. Jason glared back at Gabe as he lingered in the dining room.

"It didn't take her long to get hooked on Barney, did it?" Gabe ignored Jason's expression and helped Tatiana carry the dishes to the kitchen.

She smiled. "Did you watch Barney when you were a child?"

"Nope. The Cookie Monster from *Sesame Street* was my favorite." Gabe patted his stomach. "We were soul mates."

She laughed aloud, and the sound of her laughter warmed Gabe's heart. He leaned against the counter and watched her load the dishwasher. "Tell me about your childhood."

Her shoulders tensed, and she ducked her head. "There

is not much to say," she said. "My brother Anton, he was two years older. We were very poor, and always we feared the knock on the door at night. *Otets,* Father, worked in a factory a few blocks from our home, and *Mat,* Mother, took in laundry and kept us out of trouble."

"Are they still alive?" His heart stirred at the sadness in her eyes.

She shook her head. "All dead. My parents died in a riot ten years ago. Anton was killed two years ago." Her voice trailed off, and she swallowed hard. "Anton and Sergio, my husband, were demonstrating for the right to worship as they pleased. A soldier panicked and began firing on the crowd. They were both killed."

Gabe winced. "That's why you're angry at God." She might not know it, but she still hungered to know what had driven her brother and husband to take a stand. He'd seen it in her eyes last week at church—a deep-seated wistfulness as she listened to the pastor's preaching.

Tatiana bit her lip. "If God exists, He is cruel. I have no wish to know such a brutal God." She turned away, but too late to hide the shimmer of tears in her eyes. It was more proof to Gabe that she longed to be proven wrong. "What kind of God would leave my daughter without a father?"

He silently prayed for the right words. Marshaling his thoughts, he sighed and cleared his throat. "God doesn't look at death the way we do, Tatiana. In Psalms it says, 'Precious in the sight of the Lord is the death of his saints.' And God didn't promise we would never have trials or tribulation in this life. He promises we will. What kind of an adult do you think Irina would grow into if she were never allowed to experience disappointment or pain, if she were never denied anything?"

Tatiana's eyes widened. "*Ploho*. Bad. She would be self-centered and impossible to live with."

"Can you just consider the thought that these present trials prepare us to take our places in our eternal home? That just maybe God is helping us to grow into the kinds of people we were always meant to be. With His help, we can rise above these things that come."

A frown creased her brow as she thought about what he was saying. "What you say makes sense. But how could a God who loved Sergio let him die in the streets like a dog? How could a loving God leave Irina fatherless?"

"She isn't fatherless, and neither are you. You still have a Heavenly Father who loves you both far more than any earthly father could."

Tears filled her eyes, and she put a hand to her mouth. "I cannot speak more of this right now." The color drained from her cheeks. "*Pazhaluysta*. Please. I must check on Irina. Tell your mother I will be down shortly." She hurried from the room.

Gabe rubbed his tight neck. Only time would tell if his words had been dropped onto fertile soil or hard ground that needed more work. And how much of his zeal to tell her the Good News was because he cared about her soul? Or did he just want her to follow Jesus so it was safe to love her? He couldn't answer that question.

eight

Tatiana pressed cold fingers against her burning cheeks. Her eyes felt gritty. Why should sentimental words about a Heavenly Father reduce her to such a state? Still, Gabe's words had hit home. She felt so alone, so bereft of anyone who cared about her. But she'd taken care of herself and Irina this long; she could continue to do so. No invisible God was going to put food in front of them.

Peeking in on Irina, she found her playing with a set of Playmobile firemen. She watched her daughter for a moment. The toys seemed somehow appropriate. Sometimes she felt like she was in a burning house, running toward the cool air of freedom while flames of poverty and hardship raced to consume her. She shrugged at her fanciful ideas.

"There you are, my lamb. Are you ready to watch your Barney video?" She sat on the edge of the bed and touched Irina's tight curls. Americans had no idea of the luxuries they enjoyed, things like well-stocked grocery stores and a selection of children's videos that was mind-boggling. And she and Irina were actually here. The thought sent a wave of profound relief through her.

Irina nodded, then crawled into her lap and nestled her head against her chest. She corked her thumb in her mouth, and Tatiana gently pulled it out. "You're tired. How about a bath, and you can watch Barney in bed for a little while?"

She bathed Irina and popped her into her footed sleeper with Pooh on the front, then carried her to bed.

Irina rubbed her eyes. "Where is Daddy? He will read me a story."

"He is busy with the guest. I shall read to you." How did she get Irina to call Gabe by his name? The longer she thought of him as Daddy, the harder it would be to make the break that had to come.

Irina's face wrinkled, and she began to wail. "He promised." Tatiana tried to shush her before she disturbed anyone downstairs, but her sobs grew in intensity. A full-fledged tantrum was brewing.

A shadow loomed at the door. "I come to read a story, and I find you wailing like a banshee. If that's the kind of welcome I get, I'll just go back downstairs." Gabe stepped into the room and put his hands on his hips.

Irina hiccuped and rubbed her wet eyes. "*Mat* said you were too busy to read."

"I'm never too busy to read to my favorite girl." He began to rifle through the books in the bookcase beside the bed. "Which one will it be tonight?"

Tatiana watched him pull out a copy of a story about Tigger. He was so good with Irina. Someday he would be a wonderful father. Too bad it wasn't with Irina and more children of their own. She dropped her eyes at the sting of tears.

Gabe tucked the covers under Irina's chin and opened the book. His baritone voice sent shivers up Tatiana's spine, and she had a strange sense that this scene would always stay in her memory—the March wind howling outside the window, the room dimly illuminated with the bedside lamp, and the sleepy face of her daughter as she listened to the man she had grown to love. The man who would never be her father, no matter how much she wished it. And no matter how much Tatiana wished it.

Gabe had just gotten to the part where he was singing the Tigger song. He sang, "The most wonderful thing about Tiggers is, I'm the only one."

Tatiana giggled. He stopped and waggled his eyebrows at her. "You don't like my singing?"

She bit her lip at his woeful expression and struggled not to laugh. "Many times you have sung that song, have you not?"

He grinned. "It's my favorite." He gazed down on the sleeping child. "She's out. Hard day for her?"

Tatiana nodded. "Your mother invited a friend to bring her granddaughter over to play. Until four they played. That hour nap she had was not enough."

He put the book on the nightstand. "You were supposed to go to the family room while I read to Irina. Guess I forgot to tell you."

"You did not tell me because you did not want me to see Jason. He seems very nice."

"He's a barracuda." Gabe frowned and took her arm, steering her toward the door.

"A–a fish?" Maybe his eyes bulged a bit like a fish, but it seemed unkind to mention it.

Gabe's lips twitched. "A barracuda. As in a fish that likes to prey on smaller fish. He's not the kind of man you should be looking for."

"And what kind of man should I be seeking?" She stopped in the hall and stared into his gray eyes. She knew the answer to her own question, and he stood before her.

He sighed and ran a hand through his dark hair. "Someone who would love Irina. Someone who would come home to you every night and not go out chasing other women."

"Someone like you." She touched his chest with her fingertips. Her mouth went dry at the expression in his eyes.

He wrapped his fingers around hers and raised her hand to his lips. "Someone better than me," he said, his voice hoarse with emotion.

"That would be impossible," she said. Her voice was a mere whisper, and she curled her fingers around his.

A muscle twitched in his neck, and he swallowed. His gaze dropped to her lips, and she knew he was going to kiss her. She felt as though she might suffocate, yet hardly dared breathe. Her lips parted in anticipation, and she tilted her chin up. Gabe ran a thumb over her chin, and she shivered at his warm touch.

He bent his head, and his lips barely brushed hers. She felt the shock of that touch to her toes. Closing her eyes, she wrapped her arms around his neck, and he gathered her close. His lips found hers again, and she sank into the kiss as into the warm waters of a tropical paradise.

He tore his lips away and thrust her aside. "No! I can't."

Tatiana staggered and touched the wall to steady herself. A numbing cold sank into her, and she shuddered. Why did he refuse to let her close? His gray eyes were stormy, and he gritted his teeth as if he struggled for control of his emotions. She could see he wanted to take her into his arms again. She didn't understand this struggle he waged.

Clasping her arms around herself, she stepped further

away. "I—I must go to your mother."

"Wait, let me explain." He held out a hand, but she evaded it.

The numbness was beginning to wear off, and she could feel the crushing pain approaching. Blinking back tears, she hurried down the hall. She didn't want an explanation; her heart couldn't take hearing the rejection in words. His actions had been blunt enough. For some reason, she wasn't good enough for the great Gabe Salinger. Well, she was good enough for Jason. *He* made no secret of his attraction. And that was enough—it had to be. Tatiana wasn't about to see her daughter hungry again.

Pinning a smile on her face, she held her head high and walked into the family room. Jason's face brightened at her appearance, and he stood.

"I need to be going," he said with an apologetic smile. "Would you walk me to the door?"

"Of course." She gave him her most brilliant smile. He stopped at the door, and she got his coat from the closet.

"I had a nice time tonight," he said. "And I'd like to get to know you better. Would you care to have dinner with me tomorrow night?"

Panic rose in her throat, and she wanted to say no. The thought of being alone with him scared her for some reason. She was being silly. This was what she came here for—a husband. He was the only one interested.

Tears burned the back of her throat, but she turned a bright smile on him. "It would have to be late. For the family I must prepare supper."

He nodded. "That's fine. I work until six, anyway. Would seven be okay? We could go to Market Street Grill."

"Yes. I will be finished by then, and Irina will be in bed."

He shrugged into his coat and winked at her. The expression in his eyes made her feel dirty, but she smiled and shut the door behind him.

"You're making a mistake." Gabe's deep voice startled her.

Curling her fingers into the palms of her hands, she turned to face him. "You don't want me, so I must find someone who does." Surely, he could hear her heart breaking.

The muscle twitched in his jaw, and he made a move toward her, then checked himself. "I would like to explain. It's not that I don't find you attractive."

She wasn't a fool. When a man found her attractive, she knew it. But she wasn't ready to hear any explanations and didn't know if she ever would be. He'd made his position clear.

Tilting her chin in the air, she marched toward the steps. "Maybe tomorrow I will listen. Today I will not." The steps seemed to stretch up forever as she mounted them. Part of her longed for him to follow and explain his perplexing actions, and another part knew she couldn't bear to hear the death knell of her hopes and dreams.

She glanced back and saw him still standing in the entry. As his shoulders slumped and his head bowed, his dejected stance pierced her defenses. He was hurting, too. But she wouldn't pity him. He had the power to change the situation. She didn't.

≈

"*Mat*, look."

Irina tugged at Tatiana's hand, and she opened her eyes blearily. The room seemed unnaturally bright. She turned her head and stared into her daughter's smiling face.

Though she should scold her for awakening her, she didn't have the heart.

Struggling to sit up, she pushed her hair from her face. "What is it, my lamb?"

"Snow." Irina raced to the window and stood on her tiptoes to gaze outside. "Much snow. Daddy says we can play in the snow."

There was work to be done, but Tatiana didn't feel like doing it. When was the last time she had frolicked like a child? She couldn't remember. Tossing back the covers, she dressed in jeans and a warm sweater. Irina was already dressed, though her green pants looked odd with the blue sweater she'd chosen. It wouldn't hurt to leave her like that to play.

"Get your boots on."

Irina screeched with delight and ran from the room. Tatiana caught her hair back in a clip and followed her. She almost stepped into Gabe. Withdrawing slightly, she flushed.

He smiled. "You going to join us?"

"Would you rather I did not?" She felt as though there was a suffocating weight on her shoulders.

He held up a hand. "Cease fire."

She tilted her head and stared at him. What did he mean?

When she still didn't answer, his gaze softened. "Can I just say I'm sorry? I would like to be friends."

Friends. She could hear the echo of pain brush her heart. She wanted more than friendship. And she thought he did, too. She'd tossed and turned in her bed last night. That kiss wasn't the caress of a disinterested man. He felt something for her. Something he was afraid to admit. And in spite of her fear, she had to find out just what had pulled him away last night.

"Then you must prove yourself," she said. He mustn't be allowed to see her heart. She wasn't ready to risk it yet.

Irina came pelting out the door. She jumped into Gabe's arms and kissed him on the cheek. "Outside, now!"

"Yes, your highness," Gabe said with a solemn wink at Tatiana.

"Irina! Where are your manners? In that manner you must not speak to an adult." Mortified heat crept up her cheeks. "Apologize to Gabe."

"I am sorry, Daddy," Irina said. "Outside now?" Her voice was contrite, but her blue eyes still sparkled. Her spirit was irrepressible.

He tried not to smile but lost the battle. "We're going," he said. As he passed Tatiana, he whispered, "Lighten up, Tat."

Her cheeks warmed at the nickname. She glanced at her clothing doubtfully. "My sweater is too heavy? But it is cold outside."

Gabe chuckled. "I mean, don't take things so seriously. Enjoy yourself. I challenge you to a snowball fight. You and Irina against me."

"You will lose. I am the champion snowball fighter." She smiled at Irina. "Tell him, Irina."

"Snowballs, snowballs," Irina chanted. She wriggled with excitement.

Gabe carried her down the steps and put her down by the closet. Opening the door, he pulled out their coats. He rummaged on the shelf and retrieved stocking hats for all of them. Tatiana pulled on the blue one and tugged the green one over Irina's curls. Gabe thrust his dark head into a red-and-white striped one.

"You look like a tall candy stick," she said.

He looked puzzled, then he laughed. "You mean a candy cane," he said. "Want a taste?" He bit his lip as though he could bite back the question.

Joy bubbled into her heart. She stretched up and kissed the edge of his chin. "Tasty," she said.

He reddened, and she laughed. Maybe he wouldn't find it so easy to put her out of his mind.

He opened the door, and she took Irina's hand and went outside. A thick layer of snow covered the ground. They had to have gotten almost twenty-five centimeters of snow. Stepping into it, the snow came nearly to her knees. They slogged through the heavy wetness to the backyard. The brilliant white made her blink.

Irina whooped with delight and scooped up a handful of snow. She packed it, then tossed it at Gabe, but it only struck his knee. Her face fell with disappointment, and she scrambled to gather another handful. Tatiana knelt and picked up an armload of snow. While Gabe knelt to gather snow himself, she dumped it on his head.

"You're in for it now," he howled. His eyes narrowed, and he advanced with a handful of snow. "You'd better pray for mercy, woman. This is going right down your back."

Laughing, she held out her hands in front of her. "*Nyet, nyet.* Do not do it!"

"Too late." He lunged at her, and she wheeled and ran.

Irina laughed and clapped her hands. "Run, *Mat.*"

Tatiana felt Gabe's breath on her neck, and she gave another spurt of speed, but it wasn't enough. Moments later, the wet snow slid down her back, and she screeched.

"It is cold!" Dancing in place, she tried to shake it out from under her sweater while Gabe looked smugly on.

"To pay for this, you will not like," she threatened.

"You started it," he pointed out. "I was prepared to be nice."

She knelt and packed a snowball together in her mitten. Crouching in a pitcher's stance, she smiled and tossed it lightly in the air.

He held up his hands. "We're even now; don't spoil it." Before she could respond, he charged her. The breath left her lungs in a soft whoosh, and they fell into a snowdrift.

He was lying beside her with his head buried in snow. Sputtering, he thrashed around until he managed to clear his eyes and mouth. "I think I came out the worst in that skirmish," he said.

She smiled smugly and spread-eagled her arms and legs. "Irina, let us make snow cherubs." She moved her arms and legs with great care.

"You mean snow angels," Gabe whispered in her ear. "You look like an angel with all that white snow in your hair. You've lost your hat." He touched her hair with a light hand and brushed the flakes from her hair.

She turned her head and stared into his gray eyes. Pulling her mitten from her hand, she touched his face. "You are cold."

He moved his head closer, and his breath touched her cheek. She shivered. His lips met hers, and she closed her eyes. The rush of emotion left her breathless. She'd forgotten the heady feeling of being in love. With Sergio, the constant battle to survive had sucked this joy out of their relationship.

"*Mat.*" Irina tugged at her other hand. "See my angel."

Opening her eyes, she blinked and sighed. Beside her, she could feel Gabe pulling away and struggling to his feet. Another moment lost. She didn't understand him. How could he be so tender one moment and so remote the next? If she wanted to know, she supposed she would have to listen to his explanation, as painful as that might be.

Brushing the wet snow from her clothes, she stood and admired Irina's snow angel. Gabe laid beside Irina's angel and made a large one of his own, much to Irina's delight. They frolicked in the snow for another half hour, but the magic was gone.

Gabe kept looking at his watch, and he finally dusted the snow from his jeans and picked up Irina. "I'm starved. Do you suppose we could get your *mat* to fix us some breakfast?" he asked Irina.

She nodded. *"Blinis!* Can we have *blinis?"*

"The batter I prepared last night," Tatiana told them. "I will get them started." Tears of disappointment stinging her eyes, she nearly ran to the door. It was best to simply put Gabe out of her mind and heart, but she was finding that was easier said than done.

nine

Tatiana's stomach knotted almost painfully at the thought of the evening ahead. She felt like a slave on an auction block about to be sold to the highest bidder. Unfortunately, Jason seemed to be the *only* bidder. Gabe had made it pretty plain that he was not a contender.

She had fed the family, bathed Irina, and sat waiting for Jason to arrive. What did she talk about to a stranger? She knew nothing about him. Twisting a strand of hair around her finger, she sighed and stared at her reflection in the full-length mirror. The black skirt came nearly to her ankles. She twisted so she could see the back. It wasn't too tight, was it? She didn't want to give Jason the wrong idea.

Her high-collared white blouse made her look a bit like a schoolgirl, but maybe that would deter any amorous attention Jason might try. Sighing, she picked up her black cardigan and slipped her arms into the sleeves. The bulky fabric felt a bit like another layer of armor to her, and the tension in her shoulders began to ease. She opened her door and slipped down the hall to peek in on Irina.

Gabe was sitting on the floor with Irina, her small face rapt with attention as he made some small movements with his hands.

"The itsy-bitsy spider climbed up the waterspout. Down came the rain and washed the spider out. Out came the sun and dried up all the rain, and the itsy-bitsy spider climbed up the spout again."

Tatiana shuddered. She hated spiders, but her lips twitched as she tried to suppress her smile. The sound of his deep voice singing such a silly song amused her. She was glad she had managed to hide her smile when he looked up and saw her in the doorway. His voice faltered, then trailed off.

He cleared his throat. "So you're going." There was a trace of surprise in his voice as if he had thought she would change her mind.

"Of course," she said. "I must."

"I told you I would see what I could do about a visa."

The hint of censure in his voice angered her. "You think I am so finger-headed that I did not check to see if I could come to the States another way? You can check, but I already know the answer."

The puzzlement on his face changed to amusement. "Knuckleheaded," he corrected.

She put her hands on her hips. "Always, you correct me. Finger-headed, knuckleheaded, it is all the same. You think I am too stupid to take care of myself and Irina!"

His smile faded, and he stood, then walked toward her. Putting his hands on her shoulders, he stared into her face. "I don't think you're stupid at all, Tatiana. If you really want to know, I think you're rather remarkable. Not many women would have the pluck and determination to do something about their situation. But, believe me, Jason is not the way."

For a moment, she wavered in her resolve to go through with the evening. Staring into Gabe's gray eyes, she wanted to fling herself into his arms and allow him to take care of her and Irina, to rest in his strength and confidence. But her rational mind intervened. She had to grasp every opportunity, no matter how unlikely. Let Gabe check with Immigration if he wanted. She already knew he would get nowhere. In the end, only Irina would pay the cost if she let a chance for a better life slip through her fingers.

She pulled away, already missing the warm press of his fingers. The light in his eyes died, and he dropped his hands. "For you, I am not good enough." Her defiance faded at the shock on his face. "I must go," she said. "Ask if you wish. But already I check it. I will not be allowed to stay unless I am married."

She went to Irina and kissed her good night. With her daughter's small arms around her neck, she knew she was doing the right thing. Already, Irina was filling out. No longer could she feel Irina's bones through her skin in a way that frightened Tatiana. She was still too thin, but with good food, she would soon look like any other American child. Her eyes misted with tears at the thought. No sacrifice was too great for that.

"You be a good girl," she admonished. She released Irina and stepped away.

"I will, *Mat*," Irina said. She went back to looking at her book, and Tatiana turned to leave.

Gabe was still by the door. "Do you have change?" he asked.

"Change? I told you I must do this."

"No, change. Coins."

"Ah." She took a deep breath. "I will have to pay for my own meal?" Alarm raced through her. She didn't have enough money to spend for such frivolity. On the heels of dismay came relief. This might be a way out of the evening.

Gabe chuckled. "No, I'm sure Jason will pay. I meant in case he gets out of line, you might need to call me to come pick you up. I don't want you to be stranded with no money." He dug into his pocket and pulled out a couple of coins, then hesitated and dropped them back into his pocket. "On second thought, take my cell phone." He pulled a small flip-top phone out of his shirt pocket. Dropping it into her hand, he took out his wallet. "And here's my business card. Our home phone number is on it. If Jason does anything that makes you uncomfortable, call me and I'll come get you."

Tatiana watched while he demonstrated how to use the phone. Such a good man. So concerned for her, so loving with Irina. Tears pricked her eyes. But he didn't want her. She tilted her chin. She would find someone who did. "*Spasibo,* thank you," she said. "I must go. He is surely waiting in the entry."

He nodded and stepped away from the door. She dropped the phone and the card in her purse and went down the stairs.

Jason was not by the door, but she heard voices from the living room and headed in that direction. He sat on the sofa with his legs crossed negligently and one arm across the back of the sofa. Grace sat in her chair across from him, and Mike stood leaning against the doorjamb.

Mike smiled triumphantly when she entered the room. "You didn't tell me you had a date," he hissed as she passed near. "Told you I'd find you a husband."

Jason stood and came toward her. "You look lovely," he said.

Her stomach fluttered at the admiration in his gaze. It had

been a long time since someone stared at her with such unabashed enthusiasm. She just wished it was Gabe who held her in such awe. *"Spasibo,"* she said. "Thank you."

He gave a wave to Grace and Mike, then held out his hand to Tatiana. "Shall we go?"

His eagerness was flattering. She smiled her good-bye to Grace and Mike, then gave him her hand and allowed him to lead her toward the door. The press of his fingers brought no flutter to her stomach, no special feeling of joy. It would come, though. She just had to give it time. She pulled her hand free and opened the closet for her coat. He helped her slip it on, then opened the door for her. The touch of his hand against her back as he ushered her into the car brought no thrill of hope for the future, just a sense of dread.

His car was a small sporty model. The new-car smell enveloped her, and she settled into the comfortable seat and fastened her seat belt. Relaxing to the purr of the engine, she leaned her head against the back of the seat.

"Tired?" he asked.

She shook her head. *"Nyet.* Just relaxed." Turning her head, she studied his profile. Not handsome, but that wasn't important. Judging from the car, he would be a good provider. And as long as he was kind to her and to Irina, she would be content. He seemed placid and stable. That's what she and Irina needed. Stability. Somewhere they could feel safe.

As they drove to town, he told her about his work for a contractor. He was divorced, which was a bit disconcerting to her. She believed a marriage was forever. But she would be a good wife to him; he would have no need of a divorce lawyer again.

He turned on Market Street and parked. The street was illuminated with old-fashioned streetlamps that added a nostalgic air to the nineteenth-century storefronts. Market Street Grill was near the end of the block, and they entered under a green awning. The place was busy, so they waited in antique barber chairs by front windows that looked out on the street.

Tatiana felt tongue-tied in such a crowded place. Snippets of conversation floated around her in too fast a swirl to even understand.

Jason leaned toward her and touched her arm. "You're the most beautiful woman here," he said.

The smugness in his voice gave her pause. Was that all he cared about? Her appearance? What about the real person inside? She forced a smile. "It is very noisy here."

He took her hand and squeezed it. "Did you want to be somewhere private? We could order our food to go and take it to my house." He raised his voice a bit in eagerness.

Alarm raced up her spine. At least, in the buzz of conversation she didn't have to face any kind of inappropriate attention. "No, this is fine." She pleated the folds of her skirt and looked away. The disappointment on his face chilled her. Did he think she was the kind of woman who would welcome that kind of attention from someone she barely knew? She suppressed a shudder. Enduring them from someone she didn't love would be bad enough after marriage.

His name was called, and Jason led the way to their booth in the nonsmoking section. Instead of sitting across from her in the booth, he slid in beside her.

Sliding his arm across the back of the booth, he smiled at her. "Comfortable?"

How could she ask him to move further away? She nodded and picked up the menu. The scent of his cologne overpowered the enticing aroma from the kitchen. It was giving her a headache.

"Well, hello there." A dark-haired man of about thirty-five stopped at their booth and stood smiling at them. His gray suit was impeccable, and his white shirt was carefully starched. His appearance oozed money. A redhead in a slinky green dress clung to his arm like a limpet, her green eyes smoldering with appraisal as she looked Tatiana's appearance over. She sniffed and snuggled closer to the man.

Jason put down his menu and pulled Tatiana closer in a proprietary hold. "Steve. I left a message on your voice mail. Those initial drawings are done. We should be ready to break ground on schedule."

Tatiana wanted to struggle away, but Jason's fingers bit into her arm in a grip that was almost painful.

Steve laughed. "You always seem to find the most beautiful women around, Jason. I can't figure it out. I must be missing something."

Jason grinned. "You don't do too badly yourself." He stared frankly at the young woman until she blushed hotly and stared back at him with an imperious air.

Tatiana's temper began to rise. She was not a doll to be shown off like a trophy. Stiffening, she tried to pull away, but Jason's grip tightened. Glancing around, she saw they were beginning to attract some attention.

"Excuse me," she murmured, "I–I need to find the washroom."

"Later," Jason hissed. His grin widened. "Would the two of you care to join us?"

"No, thanks," Steve said. "I intend to have Monica all to myself." He squeezed his date around the waist and waved a hand in farewell. "I'll talk to you Monday."

He hadn't even introduced her. Steve hadn't introduced his date, either, just referred to her as though she were a possession. If there were any hope of relationship with Jason, Tatiana would have to make sure he understood such behavior was not acceptable.

"Guess I showed him," Jason said. His smug expression spoke volumes. "I was proud to have you here with me." He snaked an arm around her shoulders and hugged her, then nuzzled her neck.

Tatiana gasped in outrage. She put a hand against his chest and shoved. "I do not even know you. You must not act so."

He laughed and released her. "I was too excited to think about what I was doing. I'm moving too quickly for you." Picking up the menu, he opened it. "Have you decided what to order?"

She released the air she'd been holding in her lungs. Her hands trembled slightly as she picked up her menu. He didn't even seem sorry and hadn't apologized. "I think I'll have the grilled mahi-mahi," she said.

The rest of the meal Tatiana was on edge. Jason sat too close and was too familiar. Her food tasted like sand, and she ate barely a third of it. Twice she had to remove Jason's hand from her knee. Would this evening ever end? She wished she'd listened to Gabe. This guy was a—whatever that fish was Gabe had called him. Or maybe an octopus, given his incessant habit of touching her. The level of her headache increased a notch.

"How about some dessert at this great place I know?" Jason said, pushing away his plate.

"I do not think I want any," she said.

"Oh, you have to have dessert." He pulled some bills out and left them on the small tray on the table.

Reluctantly, she followed him out of the booth. She just wanted to go home, but it seemed the evening was not over yet. Jason helped her into her coat and took her hand and led her out of the restaurant.

The cold March wind cut through her wool coat, and she gripped the neck of the coat with one hand. They crossed the street and walked a block, then turned on Canal Street. An imposing brick facade with fancy painted trim was halfway down the street, and Jason stopped in front of it. The doorway was dark, but he fumbled in his pocket for a key and opened the door.

"What is this place?" She pulled back from his grip.

"My loft apartment. I have some great cheesecake in the freezer. You'll love it."

The pleased expression in his eyes made her want to hit him. He thought he had her cornered. "No, thank you. Please take me home."

His smile faded, and he stared at her through narrowed eyes. "Have you been leading me on?" he asked.

Leading him on? What did that mean? She bit her lip as she tried to decipher the meaning. He had been leading her down the street; she had merely followed.

He gave a short laugh that held no mirth. "You women are all alike. You just want a man to foot the bill without having to give him anything in return.

She winced at his bitterness. Perhaps he was merely

hurt. "You seem like a nice man, Jason. But I do not know you well enough to go to your home."

His expression grew cajoling. "How better to get to know me than to spend some time with me?" He took her hand again and tugged her toward the dark doorway.

It would be all right. He merely wanted to show her his apartment. She let him pull her for a moment, but as soon as she stepped through the door, he put his arms around her and pulled her into a suffocating embrace.

"Nyet!" She jerked her head away and pushed against his chest.

He tightened his grip. "It's okay, sweetheart," he murmured. "I'll be glad to marry you if you just prove yourself to me tonight."

As the meaning of his words penetrated, Tatiana fought more frantically and succeeded in breaking free. She fled out the dark hall and under the streetlight. He called after her, his voice angry, but she didn't stop. Running back the way they'd come, she just wanted to find other people and bright lights. Tears flooded her eyes and trickled down her cheeks.

Jason didn't pursue her. She turned onto Miami Street and hurried toward Market Street. She would call for a cab. Gabe wouldn't have the satisfaction of coming to pick her up. She would go home, and he would never know Jason hadn't brought her.

The restaurant didn't have a phone book, and she wandered down the street looking for a phone booth with a book. When she couldn't find one, she went inside J and K Pet Store. When she asked about a pay phone, a smiling young woman behind the counter offered to let her use the store's phone book. But when she tried to find a cab list-ing, there was none. She asked the clerk if she knew how to reach a cab service.

She laughed. "Honey, this is Wabash. We don't have any cabs here. You either walk or call a friend."

Tatiana's shoulders slumped. She didn't have a choice. Her fingers shook as she dug in her purse and pulled out the card and phone Gabe had given her.

He answered on the first ring.

She might as well get it over with and admit she was wrong. "Gabe, you were right. Jason was a–a fish. What was that word you called him?"

"A barracuda." She heard the smile in his voice. "Where are you? Are you all right?"

"At the pet store. And my pride only is hurt."

He laughed. "That seems appropriate, somehow. I'll be there in ten minutes."

He hung up, and she went to watch for him from the window. He was there in seven minutes. Relief flooded her when she saw his Jeep pull up outside. Until that moment, she hadn't realized how afraid she was that Jason would find her. She waved good-bye to the lady behind the counter and hurried outside. She slid inside the Jeep and slammed the door. Turning to find Gabe's gaze on her, she burst into tears.

"What did he do?" His voice was grim.

"Nothing." She cried harder than ever.

Gabe gripped the steering wheel so tightly she wondered if he might break it. "Did he hurt you?"

She sniffed and wiped at her face with her bare hands. Forcing a smile, she took a deep breath. "No, but he was not a nice man."

"No, he's a fish, remember?"

She stared at him. How could he laugh? Then her mouth quirked, and she giggled. Covering her mouth, she tried to stop, then Gabe sucked his cheeks in and scrunched his lips in a fish imitation, and she lost the battle. She laughed until she cried. Gabe laughed, too, a great belly laugh.

He wiped his eyes. "Woman, I have to get you home or Mother will worry we've had an accident."

She hiccuped and nodded. "I must check on Irina."

He gave a final chuckle, then put the Jeep in gear and pulled out onto the street.

"Thank you for coming to fetch me," she said after a long silence.

"You're welcome. I should have prevented you from going in the first place." His jaw tightened. "And I will have a little talk with Mike. He's not a good judge of appropriate men. I will have to take the project in hand myself."

Sadness pierced her heart. For all their comradery, nothing had changed. He was still certain there could never be anything more than friendship between them. But she was ready to hear the reasons now. She wet dry lips and swallowed hard. Her heart pounded, and she felt as though she couldn't breathe. Maybe she was ready to hear.

Taking a deep breath, she spoke softly. "I–I can listen now. To—to your reasons." Would she have to say more or would he understand?

The muscle in his jaw twitched, and he sighed as he realized what she meant. He reached the driveway to his home and pulled in, then stopped. The outside light illuminated his face, and his gray eyes were sober and intent. "I have to tell you that I've never been more attracted to a woman than I am to you, Tatiana."

"Then why?" she burst out.

He sighed. "I don't want to hurt you," he said softly.

"I fear it is too late," she said. "Always, we cannot go through life without some pain. We would be afraid to live if we worried about that."

"There can never be more than friendship between us. You're not a Christian."

She stared at him. "Why should that matter? Do you think I am not good enough for you? I am a good person, Gabe. Surely, you have seen this?"

He nodded. "You're a wonderful woman, Tatiana. But the Bible specifically tells me I cannot be unequally yoked together with an unbeliever. It causes too much strain in a marriage, and your lack of faith could cause me to lose my fervor for God."

"You love your God so much?" She could see there was no changing his mind. He had thought this through and knew what he must do. For a moment, she was tempted to go to church with him tomorrow and pretend a faith she didn't feel, but she knew she couldn't be so deceitful with him. Never with him. They had begun their relationship with honesty when he told her the truth at the airport, and they had to continue with honesty or there was no real caring between them.

He nodded. "He's the most important thing in my life. And I want to be able to share that with my wife and children."

"I would not hinder your religion." She knew her desperate words would make no dent in his resolve, but she had to try.

"You wouldn't mean to, but you would. There would be small innuendos at first that would spiral down to outright derision and mockery. I've seen it in the marriages of others. We must pull together in a marriage, or we would pull apart. And I mean to marry only one time."

"You speak as though we were oxen. Being yoked and pulling together." She tried to lighten the somber moment to keep from bursting into tears. This was the one thing she couldn't fight against.

He gave a slight smile, but it was tinged with sadness. "I wish it was different, Tatiana. You don't know how much I wish it."

The ache in her heart told how much she wished. He must not know how involved her emotions were already. "I must check on Irina. *Spasibo*. Thank you for your honesty." Fighting tears, she opened the Jeep door and hurried inside. His words had been the death knell of the hopes she'd cherished.

She heard him say her name, but she didn't pause. Racing up the steps, she tore down the hall and reached the sanctuary of her room. Minutes later, she heard him knock softly at her door, but she didn't answer. She didn't want him to see how devastated she was. Once she heard his door close, she slipped out to check on Irina.

Irina lay sleeping with one arm around her Pooh. The moonlight touched her face with silver, and she looked happy and content. Tatiana vowed to keep it that way. No matter what she had to do.

ten

"I knew I would not be allowed to stay without a husband," Tatiana said calmly.

How could she be so unperturbed? Gabe eyed her uncertainly. He hadn't been able to concentrate on his work all afternoon once he'd received the call. "I've called everyone I know to call. This seems to be the end of the line. There's no way you can stay without a husband."

She nodded. "I told you it would be this way, Gabe."

"He always was the stubborn one," Martha put in. Her leg was propped on a chair as she sat peeling potatoes at the table. "Mike pretty much went with the flow, but not our Gabe. He had to take on the world. Always thought, if the rules were wrong, he'd fix them."

Gabe suppressed a sigh. Since Martha came home three weeks ago, Tatiana had been regaled with every story Martha had been able to dredge from her memory.

"So, I guess I'd better see what we can do to find you a husband." The pain in his heart at the thought of her marrying someone else nearly took his breath away. How could he bear it? But it was either that or disobey God. The thought of disobedience was tempting, though. As tempting as Tatiana's beauty, as tempting as Irina's sweetness and gentleness, as tempting as his own attraction to Tatiana. But some part of him wouldn't allow it. It would be like throwing all he believed out the door.

But maybe he was looking at it wrong. God commanded Christians to feed the hungry. He could take these two he loved and keep them safe and fed. But as quickly as the thought came, he pushed it away. He was trying to rationalize it to get what he wanted, not what God had commanded. He'd seen others do that same thing, to their eventual sorrow.

A shadow darkened her eyes, and she nodded. "I must find a husband. The problem is in the accomplishing of it."

The pain in her voice tore at his heart, and he questioned his resolve yet again. He couldn't in good conscience find her a Christian man. Yet the thought of her marrying someone who wouldn't tenderly try to lead her into the paths of faith hurt, too. He sighed. "We'll have a party, and I'll invite all my business acquaintants. There will surely be someone you'll like."

"When shall we do this?" She put the roaster in the oven and turned the temperature knob.

"The sooner the better. We only have seven weeks." Seven weeks before she would be lost to him forever. Seven weeks before he no longer heard the trill of her laughter, the way she pronounced his name, the sound of her voice as she read to Irina. Seven weeks before the house fell silent with reproach. No more squeals of delight from Irina, no more Barney music, no more tiny arms around his neck. The thought was almost more than he could bear. How could it be wrong to keep them safe, to keep them here with him?

But he knew it was. He'd never fully understood the passage in the Bible about how a Christian had two natures that war against one another. The battle was fully engaged in his soul, but he knew he had to make sure God's man won. Hard as it might be.

Tatiana was rattling off a list of food she might prepare. "Fix whatever you want," he told her. "This will be an opportunity to show off your culinary skills to some lucky man."

She nodded soberly, then turned to knead the bread that was raising on the butcher block island. He left her and Martha discussing the menu and went to tell his mother. She was in the backyard getting her flower beds ready for spring.

Her hands encased in pink flowered gloves, she knelt in her garden bed turning the wet soil. She showed Irina how to dig the earth with a garden fork, then let the little girl do it for herself. Pushing a strand of hair from her eyes, his mother straightened up and pressed a hand in the small of her back. "Just in time, Gabe. Turn the hose on for me. I forgot it."

He nodded, stepped to the faucet, and twisted the handle. His mother loved nothing more than getting her hands dirty in the garden. She was like a little kid making mud pies. In fact, Irina seemed to be picking up her green thumb. Irina's hair glimmered with gold lights from the April sunshine, and she seemed in her element. Chattering happily, she dug her small hands into the earth. He watched them together for a moment. They loved one another; that much was obvious.

He knelt and began to help them. "We're having a party," he said.

Grace nodded. "I wondered when you would think of that." She glanced down at Irina, playing happily in the dirt. "I'm going to miss them both."

"You think I'm not?" He lowered his voice when she winced and motioned toward Irina. "I'm trying to do the right thing here, Mother."

She laid a hand on his arm. "I know you are, Gabe. And you're right, of course. But it's so hard." She glanced again to Irina. "I pray daily for them both. I had so hoped Tatiana would become a Christian. But life isn't always easy; the right choices are sometimes the hard ones."

"This is one choice I'm struggling with."

"We have to remember He loves them more than we do." Tears shimmered in her eyes, but she blinked them away and knelt to dig in the soil again. "I'd always hoped for so much for you, Son. Tat—well, Tatiana seemed perfect. You've been alone so long."

And he would be alone a lot longer. He sighed and went to the house. He would have his secretary send out the invitations tomorrow.

ja

The next few days sped by. Tatiana had been allowing Irina to accompany the family to church but refused to come herself. Gabe didn't push her. He knew she resented God for Sergio's death. He didn't know how she felt about what God said about being unequally yoked, but he suspected the knowledge had strengthened her belief that God didn't care anything about her.

The house bustled with preparation for the party for several days. The day came much too quickly. Gabe dressed for the party with his stomach knotted with dread. The aroma from the kitchen had been tantalizing all day, but he didn't see how he could eat anything, no matter how good it smelled. His mother had insisted on buying Tatiana a new dress, and the two had been ensconced in her room for the past two hours.

He glanced at his watch. Almost time for the guests to begin to arrive. They'd hired two teenagers from the church to act as servers so Tatiana would be free to mingle with the guests. Straightening his tie, he opened his bedroom door. He felt a bit like he was about to witness a death tonight. And in a way it was. The death of his dreams and hopes.

He went to the living room. His mother and Tatiana had decorated the room with masses of spring flowers. Candles burned in the windows and around the room on tables, their festive aroma adding to the gaiety. It only depressed Gabe further.

Mike sat on the sofa with his feet on the coffee table. He saw Gabe's frown and put his feet down. "Smile, Gabe. You look like you're going to a funeral, not a party."

Gabe made a feeble attempt to grin. Mike frowned and opened his mouth to speak but instead let out a croak of amazement. He was looking at something behind Gabe. Gabe turned, and his jaw dropped, too.

Tatiana wore a dress in a blend of soft blues and yellows. It fell nearly to her ankles in a soft whirl of color. The dress exposed her shoulders and long neck. Her hair was piled on her head in a profusion of curls, and faint pink stained her cheeks. She took his breath away.

"Do I look all right?" she asked. Her blue eyes were anxious, and she smoothed the skirt of her dress nervously.

Mike jumped from the couch and bowed. "I'll marry you; just name the day," he said.

The pink in her cheeks deepened. "Your proposal is what got me in this position," she said severely. She took a deep breath, and her gaze sought Gabe's.

"You look beautiful," Gabe said. "Like a spring flower

or cotton candy."

Mike grinned. "I didn't know you were so poetic, Brother."

His mother frowned at his levity. "Mike, I need your help in the kitchen a moment."

"Uh-oh, I'm in for a scolding," Mike said. He winked at Gabe and Tatiana, then followed Grace from the room.

Tatiana looked down at the floor. "I wish we did not have to do this. This feeling of being on display, I do not like."

"You'll have fun. All those men toadying up to you."

She shuddered. "I hate toads."

He chuckled. He loved the way she confused words, her fresh approach to life. In that moment, he realized it wasn't attraction he felt to her—it was love. The revelation staggered him. The struggle not to love her had been so fierce, he hadn't realized he'd already lost the war.

"Why do you look at me so?"

Her blue eyes were questioning, and he realized he'd been lost in her gaze. He cleared his throat. "Sorry." Turning away before she could question him further, he thrust his hands in his pockets and strolled around the room. Everything looked ready. The two teens from church hovered in the hall to answer the doorbell, and the appetizers sat on the table ready to be served.

Hopelessness welled up in him. This would be the hardest thing he'd ever done. He had to let her walk right out of his life when all he wanted to do was hold her tight and listen to her sweet voice the rest of his life. *Why, God? Why did You bring her here for me to love when You've clearly said I can't love her?*

The doorbell rang, and he turned. Tatiana paled, and her

gaze fastened on his face. He smiled encouragingly. "Randi and Tori will get it. Just relax and be yourself."

A bit of color came back to her cheeks, and she nodded uncertainly. She took a deep breath and straightened her shoulders. "I am ready."

I wish I was. The thought tightened his stomach, but he couldn't let her see his anguish. She didn't care for him the same way—she merely saw him as a way out of her difficulties. Any man would do. Though he told himself this, in his heart he knew that wasn't the truth.

The next three hours were agony for Gabe. He smiled and introduced Tatiana to all his associates. The single men were immediately interested, and even some of the married men looked her over more than he liked. The women were friendly, but there was a wariness about them when they heard she was available. By the time the evening was over, his face hurt from smiling, and his heart ached with impending loss.

When the last guest left, he dropped onto the sofa and groaned. "I didn't think that would ever be over."

Tatiana's eyes were bright, and she looked as fresh as when the party started. "This was a good idea, Gabe. I have cards from three men and a date tomorrow."

"Who?" he asked. Though he should be glad for her, jealousy stirred.

"Robert Landis is taking me to a movie and dinner tomorrow."

He nodded. "Robert is a good man, though a bit stern and sober. He has a four-year-old son he's raising alone since his wife died of cancer. If his devotion to his first wife is anything to go on, he would treat you well. He's the one I would pick for you. Just last month he told me he'd like to marry again."

"He told me of his first wife. Poor man." Her voice was full of sympathy.

A shaft of jealousy pierced Gabe's heart. She was slipping away from him. Tonight was the beginning of the end of their relationship. He didn't think he could be just friends with her when she married someone else.

He couldn't let her go without spending some time with her first. The memories of time spent with her would have to sustain him through the long years ahead. "Will you go to church with me tomorrow? I'll take you and Irina out for dinner in Kokomo, and we'll go shopping."

"Bribery?" She lifted her eyebrows, but her smile didn't dim.

He shrugged. "I'll use whatever's necessary."

She laughed. "I will go."

"You will?" He recovered enough to try to hide his surprise. "I mean, that's great!"

"I am not a complete infidel, Gabe. I will admit I am curious about how your God can exert so much power on a man that he would throw his life away like Sergio did."

He noticed she made no mention of God's influence in his own life. It was just as well. He didn't know how much temptation he could take. If she questioned his resolve again, he might not be so strong.

He put a friendly arm around her and walked her to the stairs. "I pray only for a wonderful life for you and Irina," he said softly.

Her blue eyes grew sad. "This I know, Gabe. I thank you for that."

Her eyes expressed regret and words she didn't utter, but Gabe could read them. She didn't understand. He didn't blame her. He wasn't sure he understood himself. Why had God allowed him to fall in love with a nonbeliever? Why had He brought this temptation into his life? He knew how Abraham felt when he had prepared to sacrifice Isaac. The only problem was once he let Tatiana go, he would never have her back again.

She climbed the steps to her room, and Gabe turned and went to the kitchen. He couldn't sleep now. The kitchen was clean and empty. Flicking on the light, he fixed a double shot of espresso and added some milk. He sat at the table and held the steaming cup in both hands, breathing in the aroma.

Staring into the dark liquid, he struggled with the situation. Why not just marry her? She would surely be saved once she was exposed to church enough. He could ask her to agree to attend church with him. She wanted to stay enough to do that, surely. He should just go tap on her door right now and ask her. The temptation was nearly overwhelming.

"Can't sleep?" His mother, her terry robe cinched at the waist, padded into the kitchen. "Um, that smells good. Fix me one?"

"Have this one. I haven't drunk any of it yet." He slid his toward her and got up to prepare another.

"I think the party went well. Did you notice Robert seemed interested? I had wished she would find someone a bit more fun-loving, but at least he would be kind to her and Irina."

His heart clenched with pain. Did she have to remind

him? He didn't answer but slowly prepared the espresso.

"You love her, don't you?" Grace's voice was tinged with sadness.

Gabe turned slowly. "It shows?"

She nodded. "To me. Probably not to anyone else. I'm sorry, Son."

"So am I."

"Have you told Tatiana?"

He shook his head. "What good would it do? She's not a Christian. And I don't want her to seek God because she wants to marry me. She has to come to Him freely and willingly." As soon as he said the words, the temptation to disobey what he knew was right fled. Much as he wanted to beg her to become a Christian so they could marry, there was too much at stake. Eternity was at stake. How could he even show her the right way to follow God when their entire marriage would be an act of direct disobedience?

"I think she's too honest to do anything else. Knowing you care might open the door for her to begin to seek Him, though." Her gaze probed his.

He shook his head. "I don't want to risk her eternal destiny on just a chance that she really understands. I have to trust God in this, Mother. Tatiana knows I care, but she doesn't know I love her. I don't want her to know, either, so don't tell her."

"Of course not." She frowned at the thought. "Are you prepared to let her go?"

He took a sip of espresso to marshal his thoughts. "I have no choice. God knows what's best. All I can do is trust Him. Hard as it might be."

"Her relationship with Robert will have to move quickly

if she's to stay in the States. I don't think I can bear to see her and Irina go back to Russia. That poor child was nothing but skin and bones when they arrived. Tatiana, too, but it was so noticeable on Irina." His mother's eyes filled with tears.

"We can pray, Mother. God will provide a way, I believe."

"Yes, yes, I believe it, too." She took a last sip of her espresso and stood. "Well, I'm going to bed. I leave the worry in your capable hands."

He chuckled. "Good night."

"Good night, Son." She paused beside him. "Have I told you lately how proud I am of you? From the time you were born, I prayed for you and Mike to be men after God's heart. You've surpassed my expectations."

The praise caught Gabe unaware. A lump grew in his throat. "I don't feel very godly right now," he said gruffly. "I'm questioning God's hand in this and have found myself blaming Him for allowing it."

"But you're still trusting. That says a lot. We can't avoid temptation, but we *can* stand in God's strength and not give in to it. Just as you are doing."

His throat closed up, and he swallowed. "Thanks, Mother. Just pray for me."

"Always, my dear son, always." She kissed his cheek, then left the room.

He thanked God for sending his mother at that moment. If she hadn't come, he might have done something he would regret for all eternity. He bowed his head and placed Tatiana in God's hands.

eleven

Tatiana checked her appearance in the full-length mirror. Her slip didn't show, there were no runs in her hose, and every hair was in place. She didn't know why she felt so nervous. Her heart thrummed in her chest at the thought of spending the day with Gabe. Just the three of them. They'd never done that before, and she wondered if it meant he was having second thoughts about allowing her to search for a husband.

Taking her purse, she opened her door and went down the hall. Irina's room was empty, and she could hear Gabe's voice in the entry below. She descended the stairs and found the rest of the family clustered near the door. They all had their jackets on.

"I am late?"

Gabe shook his head. "We're just eager for breakfast. Your daughter informs me she is starving to death."

Tatiana laughed. "Already, she knows how to get your attention. Look at the little piggy. She is getting fat on this good food." She poked Irina, and the little girl giggled.

"Oink, oink," Mike snickered.

"I'm not a piggy, *Mat*," she protested.

"Squeal, little piggy." Tatiana tickled her, and she obliged with an earsplitting shriek.

Martha was in her wheelchair, and she sniffed. "Manners, that child needs manners."

Tatiana stopped and raised her stricken gaze to Gabe's. He winked at her, and her heart lightened. It was just Martha's ill humor. The rest of the family loved Irina—she could read it in their eyes.

She got her jacket and followed Gabe and Grace out the door. Mike maneuvered Martha's wheelchair through the doorway. Tatiana hesitated when Gabe walked toward his Jeep.

"You're coming with me," he said. "Mike will take Mother and Martha."

Tatiana had wondered how Gabe had convinced Mike to come to church this morning. She smiled at the thought of not having to share Gabe. She took Irina's hand and led her toward the Jeep. Gabe lifted Irina into the car seat, and Tatiana got in the front seat with him.

They stopped for a quick breakfast, then headed out of town to church. Tatiana's palms were sweaty as she got out of the car. Why did anything to do with Christianity bother her so much? It was just another religion. There were hundreds in the world. This one was no different.

But as she listened to the message that morning, she began to wonder for the first time. Pastor Parks spoke so eloquently of God's love and how Jesus was the only way to God. Mohammed was dead, Buddha was dead, and so were all the others who had started religions. Only Jesus had risen from the dead.

And Christians seemed different. The people at this church seemed to really care about her. She was exhausted from talking and shaking hands by the time she left church. Had she been wrong to believe all her parents had taught her? Wrong about Sergio, wrong about God? When she was ready, she would ask Gabe questions. But not yet. He would think she was only interested because she wanted him to marry her.

Gabe seemed to sense her mood and had little to say as he turned on U.S. Highway 24 and headed toward Kokomo. This was the first time Tatiana had been out of Wabash since that first week when Grace took her to Fort Wayne to shop for clothing. The countryside was turning green, farmers were beginning to work their fields, and the scent of freshly plowed earth wafted to her nose. She rolled her window down a bit to enjoy the fragrant scent.

"Will I be here when the roses bloom?" she asked quietly. The possibility that she might not be was disquieting.

Gabe didn't answer right away. "You have a date with Robert tonight," he said finally. "Are you losing hope?"

"Maybe this is true," she said. "Disappointment has never failed me, but hope has often betrayed me. Hope seems to slip away from me like an outgoing drift."

"Tide," he corrected. He smiled as he usually did when he corrected her, but his eyes were still sad.

"Tide," she amended.

"I want you to know that I won't abandon you and Irina, even if you have to go back to Russia. I'll make sure you have enough money for food and housing." His knuckles were white where he gripped the steering wheel.

Grief touched her. He was a good man. If only Gabe realized it wasn't his money she wanted. Her heart ached. Did he still think of her as a gold digger? "Your money I cannot take," she said quietly. "We will be fine. I am a good cook, and I will find another job. But I have not given up yet. There is still Robert and the others."

He nodded as if her answer was what he expected. "Robert will be lucky to have you." His cheerfulness sounded forced.

They reached the city, and stopped at a locally owned Italian restaurant. Throughout the rest of the afternoon, Gabe didn't refer to the subject again. They laughed at Irina's spaghetti-covered face and hands, then went to the mall where he bought Tatiana and Irina jeans and matching Pooh denim shirts. They drove back to Wabash in companionable silence.

"Thank you for the day," she told him when they stopped outside the house. Irina was asleep in the back.

Pain flickered across his face and was gone so quickly she wasn't sure it was even there. He nodded soberly.

Tears choked her, but she bit her lip and struggled not to let him see. He was pulling away again, remote behind his smile. What could she do to break through that wall, to convince him they could have a good life together? Nothing. She could do nothing to change his mind. "I must ready myself for the date with Robert."

"Go on in. I'll bring Irina."

She opened the door and ran inside before she disgraced herself by crying in front of him. Tears wouldn't help now.

Robert had said to dress casually, so she put on her new jeans and shirt. It still felt odd to wear jeans. She'd always worn pants only once in a while, opting for skirts and dresses most of her life. When she was ready, she peeked in on her sleeping daughter, then went downstairs to wait for Robert. Gabe was nowhere to be found, and she breathed a sigh of relief. The less she saw of him from now on the better.

Mike was drinking coffee in the kitchen. He raised his cup. "Join me for coffee?"

"Little time I have. Robert will be here any minute."

"You're going through with it, eh? I'd hoped you would talk some sense into that brother of mine today. He loves you, you know."

For a moment her heart sang with hope, then reality pricked her. She shook her head. "He cares about me, but it is not love. Otherwise, he would not urge me to marry another."

Mike snorted. "You don't know Gabe and his religion. He takes it very seriously. If God told him to jump off Wabash Street Bridge, he'd do it."

"You do not believe." She was beginning to see more and more clearly that faith was at the heart of the differences between the men. One was weak and undependable, the other was caring and strong, like a rock.

Mike fell silent. "I know there is a God, but I have never been very good at being told what to do. Obedience is not a strong suit of mine. But lately, I've been thinking. . ." His voice trailed off, and he stared into his coffee.

"I, too, have been thinking," she said softly.

His gaze jerked to her face, but she turned and walked toward the door. "I must watch for Robert," she said. He started to say something, but Tatiana didn't wait to hear more objections. She'd had all she could bear today. All the words in the world wouldn't change the reality of her situation. She just had to live with it.

The doorbell rang, and she pinned a smile to her face and hurried to answer it. The next few weeks would decide her fate. Hers and Irina's. She would do what she must.

Robert was the only man on her horizon at the moment. She had to show him she could be the wife he needed, the mother his son needed. As long as he was kind, she would make it work. It was her duty to her daughter.

❧

Three weeks flew by. Robert occupied every spare minute, and Tatiana's spirit ranged between hope and despair. Robert was her only hope to keep Irina safe, but her heart still yearned after Gabe, no matter how often she reminded herself he was not an option. She tried not to think of Gabe. It wasn't fair to Robert.

Robert seemed kind. He made no bones about the fact that he didn't love her but instead sought only a compatible partner. Though he was a bit more stern with his son than she liked, that was likely merely the effect of having no woman in the house. She could temper his expectations once they were married. If he ever asked.

She was preparing vegetable soup in Robert's pristine kitchen. He set the table, then came to help her with the final preparations.

"You've only got three weeks left, is that right, Tatiana?" Robert ladled vegetable soup into four bowls and handed two to her to carry to the table.

Tatiana took them woodenly and walked to the table. It looked as though he would require little prodding. "*Da*, three weeks," she admitted.

So far, Robert had made no mention of anything more than the easy camaraderie they enjoyed together. She could talk to him and felt relaxed in his company, but the few times he'd kissed her, there had been no sparks. Oh, it had been pleasant enough, but reading a book or watching a movie was pleasant. She wanted more than a make-believe relationship—she wanted love. It would have been better never to have met Gabe. Maybe then she could be satisfied with only a facsimile.

"We'll have to discuss it after supper," he said softly.

She read the intent in his eyes. He had made up his mind. This was what she wanted, what was necessary. Why, then, did she feel like weeping? She forced a smile. "It is time."

He stepped to the door and called the children. Steven, Robert's four-year-old son, ran into the room followed by Irina. The children were giggling, and Tatiana smiled. Their children got along as well as she and Robert did. At least, that was one part of the tangle that seemed to be right. She lifted Irina into a booster seat, then did the same to Steven. Dressed in a smaller version of Robert's own attire of impeccably pressed pants and button-down collared shirt, he had his father's hazel eyes and dark hair. She wished Robert had his son's impish smile and carefree attitude. Robert was so serious. She couldn't imagine him making snow angels.

She ate slowly, not eager for the coming conversation. What should she say if Robert told her he loved her? She didn't love him. The truth might hurt him, but she couldn't lie. But he couldn't love her—he didn't act like a man in love. She was a convenience and a friend, nothing more. Clinging to that thought, she pushed her bowl away and went to the bathroom for a washcloth to clean up the children.

The clinical feel of Robert's kitchen and bathroom had always amused her. Tiled counter and floor wiped clean of even a speck of hair or dirt, a plain navy shower curtain with no valance, white horizontal blinds at the window, and no pictures or other decoration. How quickly she had adjusted to the warm elegance of her bathroom at the Salinger home. The pale yellow and blue color scheme cheered her up just to walk in. Baskets held towels and toiletries, a plush carpet graced the floor, and the walls were decorated with watercolor prints.

This sterile bathroom evoked very different emotions. She opened the sink cabinet. All the towels and washcloths were white. The contents of the cabinet were neatly arranged. Such fussiness was unusual in a bachelor. She hoped she could live up to his expectations.

He had put the dishes in the dishwasher and wiped the table by the time she got back. She washed up the children and sent them to Steven's room to play. The kitchen had been restored to its pristine condition before she could help.

Robert smiled tentatively and held out his hand. "I'll put on some music." He led her to the living room. She sank onto the couch while he rummaged in his cabinet. Moments later, the sweet sound of Bach filled the air. That was one thing they had in common—they both loved classical music. It was a start.

He came toward her, and she tried to smile. Why did she feel so sad, so lonely? Was this what her life would be from now on? Turning her head so he wouldn't see the shimmer of tears, she picked up a catalog and began to flip through it.

Robert sat beside her and took the catalog from her. He took her hand, and she turned to meet his gaze. The time had come. Her heart thundered in her ears. Panic rose in her chest, and she wanted to leap to her feet and flee out of the house. But she couldn't do that. For Irina's sake, she had to sit and prepare to accept what came next.

"You look terrified." Robert chuckled, but it was a half-hearted attempt at levity. "I have to admit to a bit of butter-flies myself."

She managed a smile. "I am fine, just nervous."

"You know what I'm going to ask, don't you?"

Tatiana nodded.

He cleared his throat. "We've only known each other three weeks. Under normal circumstances, I would not even consider asking you to share my life until we'd dated at least a year. But these are not normal circumstances. I can't let you slip away because I'm too timid to speak up." He smiled and squeezed her hand. "I'd like to marry you, Tatiana. We get along well together, and I believe we could make a match of it. I know this isn't the grand passion for either one of us. We've had that in our first marriages. I know you don't love me, nor I you, the way we should, but sometimes, other things are more important. Like our children. Steven needs a mother, and Irina needs a father."

Relief flooded her. He didn't expect tender words of love. She could promise to be friends. She nodded. "It is enough. I will care for Steven as I do Irina. We will have a good life." The last words were spoken as much for her peace of mind as for Robert's.

His shoulders relaxed, and he raised her hand to his lips. "When do you want the marriage to take place?"

She couldn't think about Gabe now. His memory must fade; she would make it so by simply refusing to dwell on what might have been. She would soften Robert's sternness, and they would be a happy family. "Let us wait until the week before my time is up. I will try to find a replacement until Martha is well."

"Two weeks, then. We'll go to the judge on Friday." He leaned forward, and his breath grazed her cheek. Bending his head, he kissed her tentatively, then with a new possessiveness.

Tatiana tried to respond, but her heart was like lead in her chest. This was to be her life; she had better get used to it.

Robert's somber expression was lit with a smile she'd never seen before, almost relief. Had he wondered if she would accept? Or was he as uncertain about their future as she was? But friendship was a good basis to build a marriage. It would have to be enough. But something in her soul still yearned for more—the strength and courage Gabe showed.

"What do you think about God, Robert?" She leaned her head against the back of the couch and stared at him intently. They had never discussed the subject. She'd been attending church with Gabe's family, but she had never asked Robert to go. Having him and Gabe in the same room was hard on her.

He lifted an eyebrow. "Where did that question come from?"

"My Sergio, he was a believer. I used to think he was crazy. I do not know now." Was he avoiding the question?

His gaze fell, and a nervous smile played around his lips. "Are you wanting a church wedding; is that what this is all about?"

Tatiana shook her head. "At New Life I have heard things. Things that make me wonder about God. Will we attend church as a family when we are married?"

"If you like. I've never been a churchgoer myself, but I suppose it would be good for business, good for the children." He tugged on his ear and looked away.

Good for business. Would God approve of a reason like that? She thought not. "I think I would like to go," she said slowly.

He shrugged. "Whatever you want."

She couldn't have what she wanted. But maybe church would calm this restless yearning in her soul for something she didn't understand. But it would need to be another church. She couldn't bear to see Gabe every week. And her heart would break when he finally brought another woman to church. Just the thought of someone else receiving his tender gazes made her catch her breath in pain. She couldn't be there to watch it.

She turned her thoughts away from that hurtful thought and smiled at Robert. "I must check the children." Rising from the sofa, she went down the hall to Steven's bedroom. Along the way, she saw the room she would share with Robert. It was as sterile and immaculate as the rest of the house. As cold and lonely as she felt inside. And she wasn't likely to find anything more in this house.

twelve

Exhaustion slowed Tatiana's steps as she waved good night to Robert and carried Irina toward the front door. The emotional upheaval had drained her energy. Only the entry light shone through the windows. The rest of the family must be in bed. She wanted to gather her thoughts before she told the Salingers about her impending marriage. Shifting Irina's deadweight to her left arm, she fumbled at the door. It swung open, and she stumbled inside.

Gabe caught her as she almost fell. "Here, give me Irina." His eyes were tender as he stared down at the sleeping child.

Tatiana shut the door and locked it. Her heart raced, and her mouth went dry. He would look into her eyes and know the truth. Could she even bear to tell him? Maybe she could make her excuses and hurry off to bed. Tomorrow would be soon enough.

Gabe was already carrying Irina up the stairs, and Tatiana lagged behind. Taking several deep breaths, she tried to wipe her face of all expression. If she could just get to her room alone, she would deal with all this tomorrow.

She flicked on the hall light and went to Irina's room. Gabe had her shoes off and was rummaging in the dresser for her pajamas. Tatiana pulled her daughter's jeans and shirt off, then popped her into the pink pajamas Gabe handed her. She heard him catch his breath, then go still.

He cleared his throat. "You're wearing a ring."

His expressionless voice caught at her heart. She pulled the covers up over Irina and turned to face him. Gabe was still staring at the engagement ring Robert had given her. It still felt odd on her hand, an extravagance she wasn't used to.

"Robert will be a good husband," Gabe said. A muscle twitched in his cheek. There was a hint of desperation in his voice as though he was eager to convince himself.

Tatiana nodded. "And Irina and I will stay in America."

He took a deep breath that was almost a sigh. "When is the wedding?"

Didn't he care at all? He seemed so passionless, so resigned. Was he relieved the responsibility for their well-being no longer fell on his shoulders? The thought hurt. She lifted her chin. If that was how he felt, she would make sure he never guessed at the way her heart ached.

"In two weeks. I would not leave your mother with no one to help. We must have time to find a replacement for me."

He nodded. "Mother will appreciate that."

Why didn't he get angry, tell her she couldn't marry someone else? Pain tore at her heart in a suffocating wave that threatened to drown her. He didn't care. Not really. Tears burned at the back of her throat. He was attracted to her, but that was as far as it went.

"I must go to bed. I am very tired." She started past him, but he put a hand on her arm.

"Are you very sure about this, Tat?"

The nickname wrenched her heart with pain. His fingers warmed her arm, but her heart was cold, as cold as tonight's wind had been. "Very sure," she said. "I must protect Irina."

He just nodded as though that was the answer he

expected. Dropping his hand, he thrust his fists into his pockets and turned toward the door. "If you ever need anything, I'm always here."

She could never ask for anything from him. The only thing she wanted from him he couldn't give. Angry words hovered just behind her lips, but she clamped them safely away. Uttering them would only cause both of them more pain. He would not change his mind. She could not change hers.

❧

Tatiana tossed and turned most of the night. Doubt clutched her with uneasy fingers. What if this was a mistake? Maybe it would be better to just go back to Russia. But when she remembered how thin Irina had been when they came, she knew she could not take her daughter back to that. All she'd expected when she came was to find a kind man who would care for Irina. Robert was all those things. Mission accomplished. So, then, why did the victory taste like defeat?

The house was still dark when she rose. She pulled on a skirt and sweater, tied her hair back, and went downstairs to prepare breakfast. The aroma of fresh coffee wafted to her nose as she entered the kitchen. Grace, still in her gown and robe, sat at the kitchen table with a cup in her hands. An empty one was on the table.

"You are up early." Tatiana's gaze went to the empty cup. Gabe's? She thought she caught the faint spice of his subtle cologne.

Grace's gaze dropped to Tatiana's hand. "Gabe told me your news. You'll be leaving us soon."

Her smile seemed forced to Tatiana. *"Da."* She didn't know what else to say but yes. Her stomach churned, and her chest felt heavy. The thought of leaving this place she'd come to love hurt more than she'd ever dreamed it would.

Grace stood and came to her side. She opened her arms, and Tatiana stepped into her embrace. "I love you like a daughter, Tatiana. I hope you'll still bring Irina to visit us."

Tears burned Tatiana's eyes, and she struggled to contain them. She closed her eyes and hugged Grace with a fierce clutch. Her own mother had been dead for over ten years, and it felt good to know Grace felt so much love for her. It was like coming home. The thought of leaving this place of warmth and acceptance frightened her.

She pulled back and wiped her eyes. "I must fix breakfast. The men will be down soon."

"Gabe is gone." Grace patted her cheek and turned back to the table.

"So early?" Her heart sank. She wanted to treasure each meal, each moment with him before everything changed, but it was like trying to hold sand. Their time would slip away one grain at a time.

Grace was silent a moment, then cleared her throat. "He won't be back for three weeks. He went to Europe."

Shock held Tatiana immobile and numb. Gone? She would be married to someone else by the time he returned. There would be no good-bye, no hope of a last-minute reprieve. A black cloud of despair nearly buckled her knees.

"Eur–Europe?" she stammered. "Why?"

Grace took a sip of coffee. "He had some business contacts he's been planning to see for some time. He'll be traveling to several countries. But I believe the reason he left right now lies with that ring on your hand. He thought it would be easier on both of you if he was out of the picture."

Tatiana nodded. "I see."

"I thought you might." Grace sighed. "I wish things had turned out differently, dear. I prayed so much."

And what good had prayer done? She bit back the question. Prayer had not changed God's mind about allowing Gabe to marry her. Questions flooded her thoughts, but she couldn't ask any of them. The pain was too raw. Part of her was drawn to this God of Gabe's, and part of her abhorred Him as the One who had ruined all her hopes and dreams.

She moved through the day in a haze of pain. Several times, Martha asked her sharply what was wrong with her that she was so fumble-fingered, but she made some excuse and got through her duties. Irina kept asking for "Daddy," but Tatiana distracted her with toys and her Barney video. She didn't know how she was going to explain his absence to her daughter. Irina adored him, and her questions would soon turn insistent.

The house sparkled by the time she climbed the steps and went to bed. She lay awake a long time staring at the play of moonlight on her ceiling. Where was Gabe? Was he thinking of her? She didn't dare to hope such a thing. He didn't love her like she loved him, or he would not have been able to leave her. Tears leaked from her eyes and soaked her pillow.

Gabe didn't want her, but Robert did. She would try to love him; she would try to forget this ache in her heart. Perhaps they would have more children. They hadn't really discussed the possibility. She suspected Robert was mainly interested in a wife who cared for his house and his child rather than one who made demands like more children. The best she could hope for was kindness and compassion.

Sunday morning found her bleary-eyed from lack of

sleep. She roused Irina and got her ready for church. She was tempted to stay home herself, but she knew Grace enjoyed her company. And some part of her was drawn to the messages she'd been hearing. She wasn't ready to swallow the story of God's love for her yet, but at least she admitted to a curiosity about it.

Mike had made his excuses again, and Martha was too tired, so it was just Grace, Tatiana, and Irina. Grace drove her Chrysler through town in silence. Tatiana had nothing to say, either. Everything had already been said. All the words in the world wouldn't change things.

৯

Somehow, she got through the next two weeks. Grace took her shopping and insisted on buying her a blue silk dress to wear to the wedding. She and Robert, along with Irina and Steven, were going to Walt Disney World on their honeymoon, and Grace bought her several outfits and five play sets for Irina, as well as some things for her new home.

She was seated on the sofa showing the blue and yellow kitchen towels to Robert when he frowned.

"I hope you aren't planning on making a lot of changes to the house," he said. "Steven and I like things just as they are. I hate clutter."

"But everything is just white," she protested. "The color, it would bring me happiness, you see?" Her heart sank at the thought of living in a world with no color, no joy.

"White is easy. Everything matches, and I can see that it's clean." His nostrils flared, and he breathed a bit hard as though he was trying to keep his temper.

Misgivings unsettled Tatiana again. What was she bringing Irina into? Would Robert's perfectionism spill over onto her daughter's behavior? Would he be critical of every little thing she tried to do?

She bit her lip. Now was the time to take a stand. "White is so—so cold," she said. "Always I like some color. Even in Russia where we are poor, I bring in wildflowers in summer and red twigs in winter. I must have some freedom to do this, Robert."

His eyes narrowed, and his lips thinned. "We will discuss it later," he said.

"*Nyet,* we will discuss it now," she said firmly. "I must know what you expect from me, from Irina."

He sighed and crossed his arms. "I expect you to care for my house the same way I would, to care for Steven with the same love and devotion you give Irina. I hated the fussiness Ellen insisted on in the house when she was alive. I don't want that again. In fact, I will not allow it."

"You allowed it with her," she pointed out.

"That was different," he said.

"You loved her, I know. But I must have the same respect for my wishes as I will give you. I would not expect you to live in chaos, but you cannot expect us to live in a—a hospital." Inside, she was quaking at the anger she saw gathering in his face. A voice of reason screamed for her to be quiet or he wouldn't marry her, but she couldn't stop now. Something drove her on. She was tired of being treated like poor trash.

Then his shoulders sagged in defeat, and he forced a smile. "You're right. I've lived alone too long. Of course, this must be your home, too. We'll work things out as we go along."

Relief flooded her. It would be all right, after all. It was as he said—he'd lived alone for too long. She smiled. "I will be a good wife to you, Robert. You will not be sorry."

He leaned over and kissed her. "We'll rub along together, Tatiana. It will be an adjustment for both of us, but we'll manage. Hey, was that our first fight? It wasn't so bad." He chuckled.

She nodded and allowed his kiss. He jumped up from the sofa and started for the kitchen. "You want to fix dinner or go out?"

She had a choice? Usually, he expected her to cook. "Let us go out," she said.

She almost changed her mind when she saw him frown, but he didn't give her a chance. "Fine," he said. Though his tone was abrupt, he sent her a stiff smile. "I'll get Steven and Irina." He went down the hall to the playroom.

Her head snapped up when she heard him raise his voice in an icy tone. Her heart skipped in her chest as she raced down the hall to see what was wrong.

"What have you done?" Cold anger radiated from Robert. Steven's hair was cut almost to his scalp, and his dark curls lay on the floor in telltale reproach. Irina held the scissors poised above his head to make another snip.

She dropped them guiltily at Robert's roar and burst into tears. "He needed a cut," she sobbed. *"Mat!"* She ran toward her mother, but Robert intercepted her and swung her into his arms.

Her tiny feet kicked in the air as he dangled her above the ground. "You must be punished, Irina."

"Nyet!" Rage held Tatiana immobile only a moment. She grabbed Robert's arm. "To me! Give her to me!" She didn't dare grab her daughter and try to take her by force

for fear of hurting her.

He jerked his arm away and tucked the wailing child under his arm. "She must be punished," he said tightly. "Look at Steven. He looks ridiculous!" His son promptly burst into tears at his father's accusatory words.

"She is my child. I will handle any punishment," Tatiana said between her teeth. Irina was screaming in terror. She had to get her out of here. "Give me my daughter."

"She will never learn if you pardon every transgression," he said firmly. He picked up the scissors. "She'll remember this if she looks as ridiculous as Steven."

Irina began to wail even louder and squirmed in his grip.

"Nyet!" Tatiana dove for Irina and managed to grasp her around the waist and tear her from his grasp. "Two wrongs do not a right make," she panted. Her daughter clutched her around the neck with sweaty fingers still holding traces of Steven's hair.

Robert's icy control didn't slip. That was what terrified Tatiana the most. His utter calm determination to discipline Irina as he saw fit, in spite of any objections. With a sudden clarity, Tatiana saw what had bothered her about Robert all these weeks—his unwavering belief that he was right, that his way was right. She and Irina would never be able to measure up to those standards. This was just the first instance of their failure.

Tatiana wheeled and dashed down the hall. His careful tread followed her. He stopped at the door, his gaze raking her face as though he'd never seen her before. "I cannot have you undermining my authority in my own house, Tatiana. We must start out as we mean to go on. Give Irina to me. I won't harm her. She must be punished, though."

Her mouth dry, Tatiana knew in that moment she couldn't marry him. Irina would wither in such an atmosphere of unrelenting expectation. No child could be perfect. No wife, either. Poor Steven. "She did not know it was wrong, Robert. You punish a child for disobedience, not for childishness."

He gave her a sickly smile. "Come inside, Tatiana, and let's talk. We must discuss who disciplines the children and how we can work together on this."

She shook her head. "I am going home," she announced.

His expression grew more dour. "If you go home now, there will be no marriage," he warned.

"Of course, there will be no marriage!" she shouted. Shaking with rage and reaction, she soothed her sobbing daughter. "To marry such a cold fish, I cannot do."

"You'll regret this," he called after her. "Who will you find to marry you in a week?"

Who, indeed? There was no one. Shuddering, she shifted Irina to her other arm and continued down the street. Behind her, she heard Robert shut the door with his calm deliberation. Her shoulders sagged with relief. At least that was over. But what was she going to do now?

There would be no choice but to return to Russia. Tears coursed down her cheeks. Failure, she was a failure as a woman and as a mother. But, no, not as a mother. At least, she had saved Irina from living with such demanding perfectionism.

The road back to the Salingers' was four miles and took her over an hour with Irina in her arms. By the time she arrived, she knew what she must do. It would be the hardest thing she had ever done, but it was the only thing that would save Irina. She had no choice.

thirteen

The house felt empty when Tatiana walked inside. She carried Irina upstairs and laid her on the bed. Her lids fluttered, but Irina didn't awaken. The ordeal had exhausted her. Tatiana felt an overwhelming wave of love sweep over her for her daughter. She would do anything to keep her safe. Anything, even what she must do now.

Her throat sore with unshed tears, her eyes staring in shock and purpose, Tatiana went to find Grace. The older woman would agree; Tatiana knew this beyond any doubt. She loved Irina as her own grandchild.

The ticking of the grandfather clock in the entry echoed loudly in the stillness. Where was everyone? Peeking into Martha's room on the first floor, she saw the housekeeper sleeping in the bed. Her mouth half open, she snored softly.

Tatiana pulled the door shut behind her and went down the hall to the kitchen. Empty. She finally found Grace in the family room. Curled up on the sofa, she held a novel. Tatiana squinted to read it. *War and Peace.* Maybe Grace was trying to learn more about Russia.

Engrossed in her book, Grace didn't see her standing by the door at first. Then Tatiana moved, and Grace looked up.

She put the book in her lap. "Whatever has happened, Tatiana? You're white as a ghost and shaking. Come sit here by me." She sat up and put her feet on the floor.

Tatiana burst into tears and ran forward, dropping to her

knees and burying her face in Grace's lap. The comforting scent of Grace's lilac sachet made Tatiana cry harder.

Grace stroked her hair and murmured comforting words. "There, there, darling girl. Tell me what's wrong. Nothing is that bad. We'll fix it; you'll see."

Tatiana cried harder. It *was* that bad. She just didn't have the words to speak it yet. Finally, her storm of tears tapered off. She raised her head and sniffed. Rubbing her swollen eyes, she sighed, then hiccuped.

"Tell me what's happened. Did Robert break the engagement? That's the only thing I can think of that would cause this." Grace's gaze sharpened, and her lips thinned.

Tatiana shook her head. She told Grace what had happened at Robert's, and the other woman's expression grew more grave.

"You were right to leave," she declared. "I would never have guessed Robert could act so badly. That just goes to show you how important it is to know someone well before marriage."

"Back to Russia I will have to return," Tatiana said. Hopeless despair gripped her.

Her eyes filling with tears, Grace nodded. "We won't abandon you, Tatiana. Gabe is determined to see that you are never in want."

"His money I cannot take." Tatiana choked out the words. "But Irina, she deserves everything." She took a deep breath to steady herself, and Grace's anxious face swam in her vision. "There is a way to keep her safe, but only you can help."

"You know I would do anything for her, anything for you." Grace smoothed the tangled hair back from Tatiana's face.

Tatiana struggled to force the words out. "I want you to adopt Irina." She slammed her lids shut and gasped aloud with the pain her own words had brought. Her heart pounded in her ears. This was the thing she'd fought against ever since Sergio had died. Irina was *her* daughter; giving her up would be the hardest thing she'd ever done.

Biting her lip until she tasted blood, she opened her eyes and focused on Grace's shocked face. "In Russia, almost, I put her in the orphanage. I could not bear that she cried with hunger."

"We would not let that happen again, Tatiana." Grace put her hands on each side of Tatiana's face.

"You would not intend to, perhaps," Tatiana said slowly. "But as time passed, our memory would fade. Besides, it is not just the food. Irina will have many things here she cannot have in Russia. Please, if you love her at all, you will do this." If only there was some other way. But she'd looked at all the angles, all the choices. Circumstances had boxed her into this corner.

Grace stared deep into Tatiana's eyes, then slowly nodded. "Very well. I shall have Mike see to the arrangements." She frowned. "If he wasn't so irresponsible, he would marry you himself."

"I could not marry him. Not when. . ." Her voice trailed off.

"Not when you love his brother," Grace finished.

Tatiana nodded. Hers shoulders sagged with relief and sorrow mingled together. It was such a jumble. But she loved Irina enough to let her go. Grief squeezed her throat until she thought she couldn't breathe.

The phone rang, and she took a deep breath. Composing herself, she picked it up. "Salinger residence."

There was a long pause, then Gabe's deep voice echoed in her ear. "Tatiana. How are you?"

She couldn't tell him, not yet. Biting her lip, she fought for composure.

"Tatiana? Are you there?" Concern sharpened his tone.

She slammed the phone down and clasped her hands together.

"Who was that?"

"Gabe."

"You hung up on him?" Grace rose and came toward her as the phone rang again. "I'll tell him," she said softly.

Tatiana turned and fled to her room. She couldn't hear his voice again. Not now. To dwell on two devastating losses at once was more than her heart could bear. Her life would be devoid of love, devoid of all that gave it color and joy. The future looked very gray.

&

Gabe's blood thrummed in his ears. Something was terribly wrong. Tatiana's voice had been fraught with pain. He clenched the phone with white knuckles. "Pick up the phone," he muttered as the ringing on the other end went on for what seemed like forever.

"Gabe?" His mother's voice was tense with concern.

He breathed a sigh of relief. For a moment, he'd feared something had happened to his mother. "What's wrong, Mother? Tatiana hung up on me."

"Oh, Gabe, I wish you were here."

He'd never heard his mother at such a loss for words. "What's happened?" He listened as she explained Robert's behavior and Tatiana's decision not to marry him. The relief that flooded him at the news left him ashamed. Was he such a sour grapes kind of guy that he would begrudge her happiness with someone else just because he couldn't marry her? On the heels of relief came sadness. She and Irina would have to go back to Russia.

"There's more, Gabe, but I want her to tell you." His mother's voice sounded frantic.

"Let me talk to her." He would reassure her that he would take care of them.

There was a long pause on the other end of the line. "She says she can't talk to you right now. That's why she hung up."

"Ask her again."

He could hear her steps up the stairs and down the hall as she carried the portable phone, then the knock on Tatiana's door.

"Tatiana? Gabe says he must speak with you."

It seemed an eternity before he heard Tatiana's voice.

"Forgive the hang up, Gabe. I was—I was upset." Her voice sounded strained over the echo of the overseas line.

"Calm down, Tat. You know I will take care of you and Irina. Mother told me about Robert." He wished he was there and could take her in his arms. She wasn't promised to anyone else right now. On the heels of that thought came that sense of God's guidance. She still wasn't a Christian. He squeezed his eyes shut and fought for control. Why was obedience so hard this time? His own desires warred with what he knew God had commanded. He wanted to chuck all he knew God demanded out the window and follow his own heart. How could that be so wrong? How could God ask this of him?

She sighed. "One day you will marry, Gabe. What would

your wife think if you sent money to Russia for me and Irina? I—we will be fine." Her voice was hollow.

There was something in her voice he couldn't read. Something she wasn't telling him. "I can come home in five days," he said. "We'll talk more then."

"You will not change my mind," she said. "This is the way it must be. Good-bye, Gabe."

She hung up before he could say anything else. The dial tone buzzed in his ear, and he pulled the phone away and stared at it. He would cancel the conference presentation. The director would scream, but he would simply have to accept the situation. Tatiana and Irina were more important. Picking up the phone, he began to dial.

⁂

Why didn't she tell Gabe about Irina? Tatiana bit her lip. She was just afraid he would talk Grace out of it, and he couldn't be allowed to do that. This was the way it must be.

"Mat." Irina rubbed her eyes and came into the room. Her curls were in disarray, and her face was pink with sleep.

A wave of fierce love swept over Tatiana. No sacrifice was too great for her daughter. Grace would care for Irina so much better than she could. And Gabe loved her as his own. Though she couldn't have him as a husband, Irina would have him as a daddy. It would have to be enough. Her throat closed, and her legs sagged. Sinking to the floor, she held out her arms to Irina.

Irina smiled sleepily and snuggled into her mother's arms. "When is Daddy coming home?" she asked.

"Soon, my lamb. Very soon." Tatiana wanted to hold this moment in her memory forever: the scent of her daughter's hair, the feel of her small arms wrapped around her neck. Through the long years ahead, this would have to be enough. This memory would warm her nights in the cold apartment without Irina. She would remember her daughter in this perfect house, with these people who loved her and wanted the best for her.

"*Mat*, it hurts." Irina squirmed.

Tatiana let her go with reluctance. Her daughter didn't understand, but maybe someday she would know what a sacrifice it had cost to give her up. Smoothing the tangled curls back from Irina's face, she smiled at her daughter through a mist of tears.

"I'm hungry, *Mat*."

Tatiana stood. "Well, we must do something about that." Never again would her daughter ask for food and find there was none to give her. Never again would she shiver in the wind with only a thin coat to protect her. The knowledge made her sacrifice somehow easier. She took Irina's hand and led her downstairs to the kitchen.

❧

The next few days passed in a haze of pain. Mike contacted an attorney friend, who drew up all the papers. Tatiana's hand shook as she signed them. She had to keep reminding herself it was for Irina. This pain was not important; only Irina mattered. It would be several months before the adoption was final, but Grace had official custody.

Tatiana packed her things in her battered suitcase. Tomorrow she would leave for Russia. Deep, pervading sadness gripped her, but she pushed it away. Though no one else might understand, in her heart she knew this was the right thing to do. She had some nice things to take back. Her friends would envy her new clothes. She set the suitcase at the end of her bed and sighed.

Going to the French door that opened onto the upper patio, she pushed it open and stepped out onto the balcony. The stars were brilliant tonight, like the shimmer in Irina's eyes when she was born. Like the light of joy in Irina's face when she and Tatiana had played in the snow with Gabe. The happiness of that moment seemed an eternity ago. Tatiana sank onto the chair and leaned against the railing. Resting her chin on her folded arms, she let the peace of the night wash over her. The pain of the impending separation struck her anew, and she almost cried out.

A sudden thought arrested her musing. Could God really love her this much? The way she loved Irina enough to let her go? On Sunday, Pastor Parks had spoken again of God's love for all mankind. It was if he had spoken directly to her. She had trembled on the verge of belief but had managed to get out of the service with her dignity still intact.

In that moment, with the majesty of the stars beaming down like a beacon of approval and love, Tatiana realized it was true. All of it. God's love, His care for her, for Sergio, for Irina. They hadn't starved, had they? Somehow, there had been enough to keep them alive. And somehow, against all the odds, she was in America with Irina. And Irina would never go hungry again. God had to have been in this. There was no other explanation.

She felt the pull toward God again. That nameless longing for a place, for a Father, for belonging to Someone who loved her just as she was, sins and all. Tears sprang to her eyes, and she gripped the railing. How had she been so blind? Sergio had been right all along. Gabe was right.

Tears spurted from her eyes in a gush. She whispered a broken prayer. "Please, God. Forgive me for not believing in You. I believe You now, that you sent Jesus to take my sin. Will you take me as Your child?"

It was almost as though she heard God's joyful, resounding *yes*. Peace crept into her heart like the first fingers of dawn. She wanted to laugh, dance, and sing. Though she faced separation from all she loved, God would go with her. She had to tell someone.

Though it was nearly midnight, she hurried down the hall to Grace's room. Tatiana knocked on Grace's door with a timid hand.

Moments later, Grace's sleepy voice answered. "Come in."

Pushing open the door, Tatiana entered and hurried to the bed.

"Is it Irina? Is she sick?" Grace struggled to sit.

"No, no, Irina, she is fine. But to tell you, I must." The joy caused Tatiana to raise her voice.

"What is it? I can see your face glowing from here." Grace flicked on her bedside lamp.

"I believe, Grace. I believe! I am God's child." Tatiana laughed from sheer happiness.

The dawning comprehension on Grace's face changed to undiluted joy. She held out her arms. "My dear girl!"

Falling into her arms, Tatiana loosed a flood of tears. At least, she wouldn't go back to Russia alone. She would have God. Never again would she be alone. The thought was heady.

"We need to let Gabe know. This changes everything."

Tatiana stared at her. "This changes nothing of my situation. I know he cares, but I would not wish to trap him. He must love me freely, without feeling he must save me from poverty. Tell him he can visit me in Russia if he likes, but I must go back now."

"Do you love him?" Grace asked gently.

Tatiana nodded. "You know this."

Grace nodded. "I will leave this in God's hands, child. He will bring all to pass according to His will."

Tatiana squeezed Grace's hand. "I know now that is best. Thank you for being a friend to me, for sharing Jesus with me." She stood and walked to the door. "I know Irina will be raised to know about God. That is more important than anything else."

She shut the door behind her and went down the hall to Irina's room. The moonlight touched her daughter's soft curls with silver gilt. She looked like an angel lying there with her cheek in the palm of one hand, her long eyelashes fluttering with some dream.

Tatiana sank to the floor beside the bed and gazed at her for several long moments. This would be the last night she would see the moonlight on her face, the last night she could watch her dreaming pleasant dreams of health and happiness. But Tatiana was content. Irina would be safe. And maybe sometimes Gabe would bring her to see her.

Tears leaked from her eyes, and she almost thought she could hear her heart cracking. She would never see Irina's first day of school, hear her excited chatter about her first boyfriend. Grace would be the one to show her how to put on makeup, advise her on her clothing and hair. All the many things she thought she would be privileged to share with her daughter would be shared with Grace and Gabe instead.

Gabe would probably marry her if he were here. Maybe it was best he wasn't. She would always wonder if he did it only because he felt sorry for her. That wasn't enough anymore. She loved him enough to let him go, too. They would all be better off without her. She carried too much baggage from the past. Let them all start fresh; let Irina begin a new life without the strains of the old life.

She kissed her sleeping child. "Sleep well, my lamb. Sleep well and remember your *mat.*"

fourteen

"What do you mean the planes are all grounded?" Gabe roared. He slapped his palm against the counter and tried to control his agitation.

The clerk's Adam's apple bobbed in his scrawny neck, and he cut his eyes away nervously. "I'm sorry, sir, but until the fog lifts no planes will be leaving."

Gabe softened his tone. Some Christian he was. He wasn't acting very trusting of God's hand in this right now, was he? "Sorry," he said. "I know it's not your fault. But it's vital I get home. Do you have any idea how long it will be?"

The clerk blinked in surprise at the apology and cleared his throat. "No, sir. The weather report shows no break in the fog through mid-morning. We can hope for that."

"I can pray for that," Gabe muttered. He gave the clerk a distracted smile and walked away.

His insides hummed with urgency. Tatiana could be impetuous and headstrong. There was something else going on, too. He could sense it. Maybe he could coax it out of his mother. He found a bank of pay phones and dug out his calling card. Dialing the number, he drummed his fingers on the side of the phone and paced two feet one way, then turned and paced the other.

Wah-wah-wah. Gritting his teeth at the busy signal, he clutched the phone in his fist, then dropped it back into the cradle. Maybe the other airport would be different. He'd try Heathrow. He went back to the counter and waited in line for the same clerk. The man eyed him warily.

"Would you call Heathrow and see if they have any planes taking off?" he asked, careful to keep his tone polite and even.

The man sighed. "Sir, the fog is over the entire area. Their planes are all grounded, as well."

"Please, humor me and check."

The man shrugged and picked up the phone. After a few moments, his boredom changed to surprise, and he hung up the phone. "The fog isn't quite as bad over there. They are thinking of closing, but so far have not. There is a plane taking off for New York in an hour. You just might make it."

"Thank You, Jesus!" Gabe shouted. "Call ahead and have them hold the plane for me." He wheeled and pelted toward the exit.

"Sir, your luggage!" the clerk shouted after him.

"Send it to me later!" Gabe had no time to worry about luggage. He could always buy more clothes. He would call his mother from the plane and find out what was going on. *Please, God, let me be in time.*

&

Tatiana cradled her daughter in her arms one last time.

"I want to come with you, *Mat*," Irina said, burrowing her face in Tatiana's neck.

Tatiana pulled her away a bit and stared into her daughter's tear stained face. She had dreaded this good-bye, but it was imperative that Irina not think she was deserting her, that she didn't want her. "Daddy will be home in a few days, my lamb. So sad he would be if you were not here."

"But who is going to take care of you? You'll be all alone

in the apartment." Irina spoke as if she were the adult and her mother were the almost four year old.

Tatiana struggled against the tears in her eyes. Irina must not know how much this hurt. "I will be fine, Irina. Jesus will be with me."

The little girl screwed her face up again. "What about my birthday?" she sobbed. "Who will bake my cake? Who will brush my hair and fix my breakfast?"

"Why, Daddy will do it. And I will bake one in our apartment and eat a piece just for you." And try not to cry bitter tears that someone else was cutting her daughter's cake and giving her presents. The thought of sitting in the lonely apartment and remembering Irina's birth brought a searing pain in her heart.

"But I'll miss you, *Mat,*" Irina said plaintively.

"I will call you on the phone and write you many, many letters. In school, you will soon be with many friends." And slowly she would forget her mother, what she looked like, the feel of her arms. The tightness in Tatiana's throat choked her, and she took a deep breath. She'd had almost four years with Irina, four precious years to love her and hold her. It would have to be enough. For Irina's sake, it would have to be enough.

Irina's tears trickled off. "Real letters, just for me?"

"Just for you. Every week. I promise." She pulled Irina into her arms for one last hug, then stood. "I must go, my lamb, or I will miss my plane." She took Irina's hand. "You can help Martha bake cookies while Grandma takes me to the airport."

"Chocolate chip?"

"I believe that's what Martha had in mind," she said.

They walked down the steps, and Tatiana took her to the kitchen.

"Well, I was beginning to wonder if I would have to bake these cookies by myself," Martha said. Her leg was out of its cast but still swollen. She sat at the table with her leg propped on a chair. The cookie dough was in a bowl in front of her and several cookie sheets waited for their turn in the oven.

Irina ran to her. "I want to help!"

Martha gave Tatiana a grim look, then jerked her head as if to say go while you can. Tatiana nodded, then hurried to the door. She paused for one last look. The sunlight gleamed on Irina's golden curls. She sat on her knees on the chair, her lips pursed in concentration as she dipped her spoon into the cookie dough and laboriously dropped the dough on the cookie sheet. Her round cheeks bloomed with excited color. Tatiana imprinted it on her memory. Choking back a sob, she turned and fled.

❧

"Come on, come on, pick up the phone," Gabe muttered. *Ring, ring.* His agitation increased. Where could they be?

"Salinger residence." Irina's high voice sounded so grown-up on the phone.

Relief flooded Gabe. They were still there. "Irina? Hello, sweetheart, it's Daddy."

"Daddy, when are you coming home?" Irina's voice was disapproving, as though she was still angry he had gone.

"I'm on my way home now, sweetheart. Listen, punkin, can I talk to Grandma?"

"No," she said.

"Why not? Is she busy?" Gabe forced himself not to be

short with her though his insides screamed with urgency.

"She isn't here, Daddy. She and *Mat* went to the planes." She gave a sorrowful sigh. "*Mat* has to go away. But she's going to write me letters."

Planes? Go away? The sinking feeling in his stomach increased. "Where is she going, Irina? You must tell me."

"To Russia. She had to go back." Irina's sorrowful tone increased. "Can't you make her stay, Daddy? I don't want her to go."

"I don't either, sweetheart. Listen, who is there with you? I need to talk to an adult." He had to find out what flight Tatiana would be on. Maybe he could stop it or call her at the airport.

"Martha is here. Here, Martha, Daddy wants to talk to you."

He winced at the bang in his ear when Irina dropped the phone.

Moments later, Martha's voice came on the line. "Hold your horses, Gabe. These old bones don't move as quick as they used to."

He wasted no time in pleasantries. "Do you know what flight Tatiana took?"

"I got it here somewhere." She rummaged through some papers. "Here it is." She read the numbers and departure times to him. "You gonna marry her? Anybody with half an eye could see you love her."

He groaned. "I wish I could, Martha. But she's not a Christian."

Martha snorted. "You been misinformed, Gabe. She's a Christian now."

He widened his eyes, and his heart jumped with hope and joy. "What are you saying?"

"I'm sayin' the lass became a Christian the other night. There is no reason not to wed her now." Martha's voice was tinged with impatience as though she thought him a trifle slow.

"Why didn't she tell me?" Another thought struck him. "And why is Irina still there?"

Martha sighed. "Tatiana had some fool-headed notion you only cared because of pity. And the missus is adopting the wee one so she can stay in America." She snorted again. "Foolish, that's what I told her. She must be foolish not to see you were sick with love."

He hadn't realized he was so transparent. His heart lifted. Nothing stood between him and Tatiana now. The flight had already left Indianapolis. He would try to have her paged at JFK in New York.

His heart was full to overflowing with joy that the Lord had found her. Found her and opened the way for their marriage. He just had to stop her from leaving. Praying for all he was worth, he settled down in his seat and stared out over the gray clouds below him.

&

The plane banked for landing at JFK Airport. Tatiana leaned over and stared at the landscape below her. Green squares, like checkerboards, opened below the clouds. Her heart felt heavy in her chest, and she was glad for the numbness. But the pain was crouching just around the corner, lying in wait to pounce like a tiger on unsuspecting prey. She had to hold it off until she was alone. She wanted no strangers asking if they could help. No one could.

The plane bumped, then the pilot threw on the brakes. Taxiing around the runway, the plane pulled to a stop.

Tatiana debated about getting off but decided to stay in her seat. The plane would take off again in two hours. Maybe she could get some sleep and forget what lay behind her. With some rest, she might be able to make plans for what to do when she reached Moscow.

Most of the other passengers stood and began to move down the aisle. Good. Maybe she would have some time alone. Time to prepare for the transition that awaited her. She took the blanket on the seat beside her and curled up under it. Closing her eyes, she drifted off to sleep.

When she awoke, the plane was boarding. She sat up and rubbed her eyes. Glancing at her watch, she saw they would be taking off in thirty minutes. She should have gotten off. She was hungry. But the stewardesses would feed them once they were in the air.

Tatiana smiled at her seatmate, then turned to stare out the window. The nap had only served to allow the numbness to begin to fade around her heart. Pain gnawed at the edge of her consciousness, but she pushed it away. She wouldn't think of Irina's blue eyes and blond curls, of Gabe's tender expression and cheeky grin. She blinked furiously to dispel the tears that pooled in her eyes.

She saw one stewardess hurry to another and whisper, then they both turned and stared at her. The red-haired one came toward her with a frown on her face. Tatiana's heart sank. Was something wrong with her passport? For a moment, she was frightened that she might be thrown in jail. She told herself this was America, not Russia, but the fear had been too ingrained. Clutching the seat in front of her with white knuckles, she watched the stewardess approach.

"Mrs. Lazarenk?"

"Yes." Tatiana's hands were icy, and she felt as though she might throw up.

"Please, I must ask you to come with me." Her voice was firm.

What could be wrong? Not sure her knees would hold her, Tatiana rose and stumbled down the aisle after her. Other passengers whispered and stared as they passed. Spots danced in front of her eyes, and she gripped the sides of the seats she passed for support. She mustn't faint.

They reached the jetway, and Tatiana followed the stewardess out of the plane.

Stepping into the brightly lit airport gate area, she blinked and paused. The stewardess stopped and turned to her. "I'm sorry to frighten you, but we were asked to escort you off the plane." She looked around. "He should be here someplace."

He? Confusion clouded her thoughts.

"Tat!"

Her head jerked around. *Gabe?* Her gaze met his. He was standing against the wall by the phones with one in his hand. He put it in its cradle and came toward her. She saw the love and joy blazing out of his eyes like a beacon welcoming her home. Her mouth went dry at the devotion she saw in his face.

He opened his arms, and she ran into them. His arms went around her, and as she felt them pull her close, she knew she'd come home. Home where she belonged.

"What are you doing here?" she whispered.

"Claiming the woman I love." He tilted her chin up and his lips found hers.

All the love she'd ever longed for was in his kiss. All the acceptance, the promise of forever she thought she'd never find on this earth. When he pulled away, she was breathless. She didn't even have to ask if he was here because of pity or duty. She knew love when she saw it.

"We have to hurry," he said. "We have a plane to catch for Indy. Mike knows the county clerk, and she is standing by to issue us a marriage license tonight. Pastor will marry us as soon as we arrive in Wabash."

"Irina?"

"She's waiting for us, along with Mother and Mike."

"Everything you have thought of," she said.

Gabe smiled. "Mike will be smug, you know. That day in my office when he told me what he'd done, I was ready to kill him. Now I'll have to thank him. I have a beautiful wife and a perfect daughter. What more could a man ask?"

She smiled. "A son, perhaps?" Her lips were tremulous at the thought of a little boy with Gabe's gray eyes and cleft chin.

Gabe touched her face with gentle fingers. "Hold that thought," he whispered. "I can't think of anything I'd like more than a houseful of our children each taking their turn in the nursery. But we have to take care of the marriage first. Let's go home."

She snuggled into his arms again. "Already home is where I am," she said.

A Letter To Our Readers

Dear Reader:

In order that we might better contribute to your reading enjoyment, we would appreciate your taking a few minutes to respond to the following questions. We welcome your comments and read each form and letter we receive. When completed, please return to the following:

Rebecca Germany, Fiction Editor
Heartsong Presents
PO Box 719
Uhrichsville, Ohio 44683

1. Did you enjoy reading *From Russia with Love* by Colleen Coble?
   ❑ Very much! I would like to see more books by this author!
   ❑ Moderately. I would have enjoyed it more if

   _____

   _____

2. Are you a member of **Heartsong Presents**?   Yes ❑   No ❑
   If no, where did you purchase this book?_____

   _____

3. How would you rate, on a scale from 1 (poor) to 5 (superior), the cover design?_____

4. On a scale from 1 (poor) to 10 (superior), please rate the following elements.

   _____ Heroine   _____ Plot

   _____ Hero   _____ Inspirational theme

   _____ Setting   _____ Secondary characters

5. These characters were special because_____

_____

_____

6. How has this book inspired your life?_____

_____

_____

7. What settings would you like to see covered in future **Heartsong Presents** books?_____

_____

_____

8. What are some inspirational themes you would like to see treated in future books?_____

_____

_____

9. Would you be interested in reading other **Heartsong Presents** titles?　　Yes ❏　　　　No ❏

10. Please check your age range:
　　❏ Under 18　　❏ 18-24　　❏ 25-34
　　❏ 35-45　　　❏ 46-55　　❏ Over 55

11. How many hours per week do you read?_____

Name _____

Occupation _____

Address _____

City _____ State _____ Zip _____

CAROLINA

Heart♥ng

Presents

Great Inspirational Romance at a Great Price!

Heartsong Presents books are inspirational romances in contemporary and historical settings, designed to give you an enjoyable, spirit-lifting reading experience. You can choose wonderfully written titles from some of today's best authors like Hannah Alexander, Irene B. Brand, Yvonne Lehman, Tracie Peterson, and many others.

When ordering quantities less than twelve, above titles are $2.95 each.
Not all titles may be available at time of order.

Heartsong Presents
Love Stories Are Rated G!

That's for godly, gratifying, and of course, great! If you love a thrilling love story, but don't appreciate the sordidness of some popular paperback romances, **Heartsong Presents** is for you. In fact, **Heartsong Presents** is the *only inspirational romance book club* featuring love stories where Christian faith is the primary ingredient in a marriage relationship.

Sign up today to receive your first set of four, never before published Christian romances. Send no money now; you will receive a bill with the first shipment. You may cancel at any time without obligation, and if you aren't completely satisfied with any selection, you may return the books for an immediate refund!

Imagine. . .four new romances every four weeks—two historical, two contemporary—with men and women like you who long to meet the one God has chosen as the love of their lives. . . all for the low price of $9.97 postpaid.

To join, simply complete the coupon below and mail to the address provided. **Heartsong Presents** romances are rated G for another reason: They'll arrive *Godspeed!*